diary of a sex addict

Praise for
diary of a sex addict

"Scott Alexander Hess's *Diary of a Sex Addict* is relentlessly erotic and divinely written."

—*Richard Labonte, Bookmarks*

"If Dennis Cooper and Chuck Palahniuk had a bastard love child, it would look like Scott Hess's *Diary of a Sex Addict*. It is bareback fiction: raw and dangerous, skin to skin and true. The next morning, we almost regret it. Almost."

—*Bryan Borland, author of My Life as Adam*

diary of a sex addict

a novel by
Scott Alexander Hess

jms books

DIARY OF A SEX ADDICT

All Rights Reserved © 2011 by Scott Alexander Hess

Cover art © Photographer: Enrique Padilla, Jr.

The stories within are works of fiction. All events, locations, institutions, themes, persons, characters, and plots are completely fictional inventions of the author. Any resemblance to people living or deceased, actual places, or events is purely coincidental and entirely unintentional.

No part of this book may be reproduced or transmitted in any form or by any means, graphic, electronic, or mechanical, including photocopying, recording, taping, or by any information storage retrieval system, without the permission in writing from the author and publisher.

JMS Books LLC
10286 Staples Mill Rd. #221
Glen Allen, VA 23060
www.jms-books.com

ISBN: 9781466258860

Printed in the United States of America

Dedication: For Ruben.

december 7

SO I'M FUCKING his face, I mean really fucking it. Long harsh thrusts that take in all my anger—the lousy job, the rattling bank account, the lost boyfriend, the twelve hundred dollar Manhattan rent—all the rage I keep sunk in my desperately shaped-up little gym ass. I'm rage-shoving it easily into his mouth. It's all I can do not to say "take it fuckhead," because I know he's dying for me to say it and I want to but, honestly, the look of his big white eyeballs and lips and fat dog-like slobbering tongue is almost enough to get me off.

    We're ten minutes into it, on the floor of my kitchenette, and I'm flagging a little, speaking in hushed tones because my studio shares a wall with the apartment of a sweet twenty-something couple. Through the wall I can often hear them chatter about Pottery Barn and Cheerios. I imagine they will hear me yell "Suck my white cock with your hot black lips." So I whisper it and he—let's call him Bing—Bing seems to really like my softer tone. But I can see his knees hurt. I touch his shoulder as he groans in what I think is pain.

Bing's skin is slick from an elegant mix of dewy perspiration and funky Ethiopian oil. Of course it could be baby oil for all I know, but I imagine it more exotically. Truth is, I know squat about Bing. We typically talk as he exit-dresses, never before. During our second fuck, it came out that he was a jeweler by day, a painter by night. Disappointing, because I had fantasy tagged him as a 22-year-old brain-damaged drug dealer on parole.

Bing has shifted, panting, with my cock in his mouth. He's losing momentum as he lifts his knees and leans back on his haunches. I am meant to follow, to stray forward to keep our fifteen minute rush of wild sex moving. Because in too long a pause, the whole delicate fantasy collapses. I do lean forward, but hesitate, realizing Bing's knees must really ache. I wonder if I'm being cruel or a bad host, which opens a peep hole into my bland, non-sexually charged thoughts and in milliseconds I wonder if the floor is clean enough to be kneeling on and if Bing could ever replace my ex-lover and why this sex right now is so mind-numbingly hot and so much better than the rest of my awful day.

I tilt my head back and for a split second glimpse, on my kitchenette wall, a yellowed image of the exploding *USS Shaw* battleship. Scrawled in the image's corner is Pearl Harbor, December 7, 1941. I need to take it down at midnight and put up my dead mother's advent calendar, something she did religiously on this date when I was a kid. The calendar kicked off her three week build to Christmas. My father, also dead, served in WWII, which is why they hung the Pearl Harbor thing in their kitchen the rest of the year. The advent calendar is cheerful and has little gifts that stick onto days of the week. This whiff of nostalgia is having a dreadful effect on my hard-on.

If I linger here, I will fall dangerously close to the sex death spot of uber-realness. Before my cock slackens and melts out of the side of Bing's mouth I thrust mega-hard and speak loudly the lines we both love: "Suck it! Love the white cock! Say you love it, fucker!" And he does say it, and I cum as expected. Not "in your fucking black mouth," but safely on his soft cheek, a few drops on his shoulder as he falls back and then. Bing leaves.

december 8

IT'S 10 P.M. Do you know where your sex addict is?

I'm slouching in a tub filled with steaming water and Mr. Bubble brand bath milk, ruminating on the fact that it's always hardest—and that is not a cock pun—it's always emotionally hardest between 10 P.M. and midnight. Why? Maybe because for years I was always stoned at this time of night. Or maybe as a boy I was finger fucked in a blackout by a fat man at this exact time. Or maybe there is an ultraviolet ray that shines from the moon onto Manhattan at 10 P.M., turning my guts inside-out and making me want to throw myself into traffic. The fact is, it's very emotionally hard at 10 P.M., and I choose sex to escape.

Having slipped in the 'throw myself in traffic' line I will acknowledge my whole-hearted love of life and schizophrenic nightly obsession with suicide. Which leads me to my black hole—again, not a sex pun, though I have lately begun fantasizing about athletically fucking Bing's hot and nasty man-cunt.

My black hole comes to life every night at 10 P.M. It looks to me like the edge of a perfectly-rounded, country drinking well. The type a rural pig farmer digs in his backyard. I see my black hole during these nightly Mr. Bubble baths, when the manic, over-caffeinated rush of my daily routine has faded into despair and drab, heavy loneliness. I see all of this now, with my eyes shut in my very hot, very soothing, very glamorously scented bath. I see the blackness and it is simple and comforting and I think, 'Oh, why not slip in, isn't that the ultimate letting go?'

It is at this point that I can either dope and drown myself, or have sex. For the drowning, I'd swallow a fat stash of post gum-surgery Vicodin (stored in the medicine cabinet) and sink forever into my imaginary black hole. I saw a film where a drunk blonde woman did this, vanishing elegantly under a veil of bubbles. So far, I have always chosen the brain-numbing sex.

So I snap my eyes open and drain the lavender scented water and douse the spring breeze candle and get ready to go study my hot little body in the huge mirror in my kitchenette.

Before I go, I watch the last gasp of soap bubbles swirl happily into oblivion.

MY MIRROR IS pretty, eight feet tall and five feet wide with an espresso wood frame. My friend Michael, a trust-fund brat who's a really talented painter, took me to Ikea to buy it. I hauled it myself up the four flights to my studio. Michael told me it would totally open up my kitchenette which it does. I knew I'd use it to study every inch of my frantically gym-tightened body and also to watch myself and nameless men have intercourse on the floor. I didn't tell Michael this. He has body issues and hates to talk about sex. This month, he's refusing to leave his house because he's supposedly gained a ton of weight. We stay in touch through texts.

The big leaning mirror also serves as a dividing line between my stove, sink, mini-fridge and a Crate & Barrel industrial, gun metal counter with two stools that I use for both desk and eating space. Beyond the counter, I've hung a floor to ceiling sheer white curtain, further separating the kitchenette from my studio's main room. This main room is dapper and elegant, decorated with an antique desk and bookcase, a leather sofa, side tables, expensive lamps and full-length drapes. The wall above the sofa features a cluster of framed artwork, a mix of oil paintings and vulgar nudes. I like to call this area my sex salon.

I'm nude now, in front of my Ikea mirror, my skin damp and glistening with the soapy remnants of Mr. Bubble. I start every day here, in this exact spot, taking pictures of my reflection to post on internet sex sites. The shots are from a distance because I look so damn lean and cut-up from far off. I do this at 7 A.M., because I am happiest at this time. The day seems possible. The subsequent hours are really just a slow motion tumbling back toward the black hole. I think Sartre said something like "Life begins on the other side of despair." He was a fucking genius, probably a sex addict.

I look at myself very closely, clinically, in my Ikea mirror. I am five foot seven. My eyes are my best natural feature because they are a peculiar shade of blue. They are pale and bright and sort of zesty. At 38, my hair is still thick and I keep it short. I can pass for 32. The super-selling point for sex hook-ups, though, are my man tits.

The day I moved to Manhattan from Fayetteville, Arkansas I joined a gym. I studied a big Arnold Schwarzenegger book filled with pictures of Arnie's smooth muscular body in a Speedo. He had a glimmer in his eye that said "I'm European and hot" though not, at that time "I'm going to be Governor of California."

I worked fiercely at free weights and moved onto studying those titillating men's fitness magazine pull-out exercise calendars where the 'straight' models grit their white teeth and flex their luscious hairless bodies while wearing really skimpy shorts. I became obsessed as my scrawny chest took shape. My biceps got that arm-curl hump and my ass hardened. That's when the sex really took off. I could put myself out there as an object—'Mr. Hot Tits'—and look for guys with equally nice pecs and asses and flat tummies. These are the guys without names and loads of energy who get turned on by the same faux porn model work-out magazines that I do.

And now, from a safe distance in my Ikea mirror, my protein-shake enhanced tits are still a perky turn on. My crotch is adequately manicured. I feel hot. Ready. Primed. Empty.

It's time to snare some big cock, and keep that depressing black hole at bay.

IT'S A DIFFICULT night. The wi-fi internet connection I raffishly steal from my neighbor just flaked out in the middle of a porn clip from *Straight Boys Suck for Cash* leaving me with a handful of lube, in utter anguish. With no wi-fi, I have to rely on the crappy internet connection on my iPhone for all of my net needs.

I normally do a triple-threat hunt to save time. This includes two online sex sites, Grindr and Manhunt, along with the phone sex line. I must have someone over by 11 P.M. and be done by midnight so I can be up at 7 A.M. to go to the gym and keep my man tits hard. Timing is crucial.

The phone sex line is the quickest and the most insane. The changing voices of the recorded messages of the men on the line sometimes frighten me. I skip through the messages randomly, waiting for a special one to yank me under. There are odd ones, like: "I just slammed crystal, I'm eleven inches and he's tied up next to me," or "I'm wearing girl's panties," then a suspiciously young voice saying "I'll do anything you want and be your bitch sir." I often nod off, the voices endless, just a run-on of desperate pleas.

But I don't stop. I wade through "suck my feet I can pay you," and "I'm straight acting and my girl's at the store," then "I eat shit I'm in my rim chair," and finally, gently "I'd really like to date."

The emotional ride I go through as I listen to these voices can be intense. I'm thrilled and terrified by the rape fantasies, disgusted by the scat descriptions but mostly saddened by the young voice with (I imagine) soft green eyes, the one that says he'd like to date and meet nice guys. I think he's mentally retarded to think he can find a real date on a phone sex line.

The phone line is chaos, but delivers men quite often. Of every ten or so, there's actually someone within a mile radius who's ready to fuck. For the record, I only have safe sex, which is, in gay terms, no anal sex without a condom and no cum swallowing. My motto: if I stay negative and safe, I get more mind-numbing, black hole avoiding sex. Being positive would really cut down on the possible number of hook-ups.

My other two hunting formats are online. Manhunt is a pic-and-click web-site of cock and ass shots and pointed descriptions about lusty desires. It's old school, like a super jaded version of match.com with long profiles, lots of pictures, and cute categories like 'top', 'bottom', 'daddy', 'exhibitionist', 'gym rat'. The success ratio is limited but not impossible.

The last and latest is Grindr. It's an iPhone application that labels men by their proximity, like *Bob is 180 feet from you, is on the down low, and likes to get spanked.* The Grindr icon on the iPhone is yellow with a bizarre skeleton mask challenging you to sign in. Once signed in, it's all sort of cheerful. The iPhone screen glows and makes it feel, in the darkness of my bed at least, otherworldly. The Grindr screen is divided into tiny thumbnail picture squares of available men, with sixteen pics filling the screen. You can scroll down with a touch, and view lots and lots of men. Pics range from a close up of an eyeball or a plump chest, to a crotch or the Empire State Building. One guy has a shot of a bowling alley lane and calls himself 'Blue Balls'.

When you tap a man's pic, you can text-chat back and forth

toward a hook-up. Grindr has the youngest, sexiest, flakiest and most confused men, and causes the worst eye strain. In the dark, flipping the screen of tiny men's faces up and down, I always think of a summer lawn, under the moon, watching lightning bugs blur past with their innate ability to exist then die in rapid blinks of light and dark. I'm not sure why. I think it has something to do with being aimless and un-tethered. There are moments of calm and frail hope. I feel less alone in the dark with Grindr.

Tonight, with the free wi-fi not cooperating, I'm lying on my pull-out sofa naked and lubed, net porn dead, dealing with the phone line and logging onto Grindr on my tiny iPhone. It's already 10:58 P.M. and I wonder where Bing might be.

I manically swap from Grindr to the phone line with no luck until nearly midnight, then fade out with the phone in my hand, its screen light slowly dimming as I see the edges of my sexless, black hole emerge. Something that looks like either a crippled hand, or a gnarled and rotting tree branch, reaches up to pull me under.

I sleep.

IN THE DISSOLVING dream there is a warm and cozy box.

I've just woken in my pitch black, hot and lush studio under my super-thick quilted Macy's down comforter, sweaty. My iPhone is quacking.

In this deep-woods dark place, under my feather stuffed down comforter hearing the phone quacking, I'm feeling very safe, steeped in some ethereal wilderness. I catch fragments of the box dream as it fades. I fit inside the box easily. It is cardboard but somehow the cardboard feels soft like fabric or skin. There is a sound of hissing, running water.

The iPhone stops quacking. I'm depressed, thinking I just missed the hottest possible trick calling in late, just a block

Diary of a Sex Addict

away, with a magnificently huge cock. The phone quacks anew and I grab it only vaguely acknowledging that I have to be up for work in a few hours.

It's not a voice I recognize so I grunt, hoping to gather information. He says he's 20, Latino, eight inch cut cock, from the Bronx and really really really wants to get fucked tonight. I give him my address then crawl back under my comforter hoping the box dream comes back. The phone call, though, woke me to the point of arousal so instead of drifting back toward sleep I am edging away from it and I realize dawn is arriving along with a flaky 20-year-old cocoa colored big-dicked bossy bottom from the Bronx. I consider popping a melatonin herbal sleeping pill.

The buzzer blares and I let him up wondering how the hell he got from the Bronx with such lightning speed, then vaguely recall him mentioning he was at a party, presumably very nearby.

I stand naked at my door in the dark. The tension is rising. I grip my penis, tugging it to life with one hand, suddenly fearful it's way too small and sleepy. I use my other hand to lift the door's peep hole so I can get a glance at my visitor before I let him in. If he's, let's says, disfigured or over 60 or holding a butcher knife, I can always stand stock still and quiet and hope he goes away. These moments, waiting for a trick to climb the four flights of stairs, I always feel a building exhilaration, titillation and also something like innocence.

It can't be real innocence since I'm such a jaded sex monster but there is a sense of discovery, and even, somewhere in my mind as I listen to the footsteps crawling up the last flight in the dead quiet stairway, a soft little fantasy from way back that this could be the one, it could be love.

I can see him through the peephole and he is exactly as he described himself. I sigh and let him in, knowing the best part is somehow already over.

❖

HE'S LYING ON his stomach on my pull-out sofa and it's very dark and he is very black. I don't believe he's Latin, maybe a mix. There are always lies with hook-ups. It's expected. He is truthfully as young as he claimed, I feel that in his voice, and though he's unshaven and has a mild inner-tube of flab around his waist, his ass is very plump and pretty. He keeps on his plastic eyeglasses and waits as I hover.

"So," he says this with a long drawn out emphasis on the 's' which makes him sound like a bored little boy, "Why aren't you fucking me?"

His voice sounds even younger, and I wonder if he's twenty or some high school kid living in a ratty housing project with a crackwhore mother. And this all somehow excites me, so I finally get hard enough to lasso the condom on and get it inside him. He props his head up on his arms and in the same monotone of boredom, though I am now pumping as hard as I can, he says, "Can't you do it harder?"

Again I imagine his mother, some fat angry crackwhore who says things like that to him, like *"Why can't you be a real man?"* or *"You are a worthless faggot."* These are things I've seen in films about poor abused children living in poverty who end up going to a college where someone like Sandra Bullock teaches them to read. I pump harder and harder. But he just sighs and finally says "If you came you can take it out. I have to go."

I did not cum, but I gladly withdraw and realize he is in charge of this scene. He gets up and dresses slowly, never looking at me. I try to prop myself up on my elbows in the dark to look masculine or cool or relaxed.

"I'm glad you came," I lie.

"Yeah, I'm sure you are," he says.

He leaves. There is a long, slow lapse where I vacantly wait for dawn to come to me but the night seems stuck. I take another melatonin pill and sleep, but I don't dream about the box.

december 9

MY MORNING STARTS with *wanna watch me be a pig, get bred by you and drink ur piss.* It's a text from, well, from him. The text-men are the toughest to keep track of. There are no pictures and no names. But this one, who's been texting for two months, always wants bareback breeding and groups and arms up his ass. I wonder if he's really, as his profile says *38 worked out hung thick* or maybe he's just a lonely old fat man dying of some horrible disease living on these text fantasies to feed himself.

I get up and wander through the dark. My studio faces the back of the building, a blessing because of the quiet, a mild curse because there is no light. I don't mind the dark because the tomb-like feeling comforts me.

Groggy, I feel hollowed out, and imagine a pretty serial killer snuck in as I slept and gutted me then filled my chest with scented saw dust before he sewed me up and covered the scars with Max Factor make-up concealer. These are typical very-early morning thoughts. I don't mind them. As I come to, I slowly recall a mean little Latino teen who couldn't be fucked hard enough, but then wonder if I dreamt that.

Two large glasses of coffee over ice and a shower and I feel better. I hang a miniscule rag doll and a toy truck with eyes on the advent calendar for December 8th and 9th and start my day. For a half second, as I turn away, I think the rag doll is laughing at me.

I look particularly smooth and chiseled this morning post shower in my Ikea mirror. I am inspired to take my morning pictures and update my online photos at Manhunt and Grindr. I can get a head start and catch the early morning cruisers, because tonight will have to succeed or else...

Or else, what? Flip headfirst into the black hole and dissolve, I suppose.

Contemplating this at the mirror, I pause to realize how horrified I am to get any closer. I don't like to scrutinize myself. It makes me feel old. My skin has been damaged by the sun and I have too many hateful freckles.

I take a step closer, feeling reckless. Another. So far, so good. Three quick steps. Finally two more and I am in it, right on it: The face. The freckled 38-year-old forehead, the crow's feet, the slight loosening of the jaw. I run back to safety where it's all about my man tits and my 29-inch waist. I study my image from five feet back and am worthwhile again, one sexy fucker.

I shut my eyes and let my shoulders fall way, way, way down for the first time in months. To make this moment seem more real, I say out loud to the mirror "Can you ever get to who you really are?" I look a bit longer at my long pale perfect nude body in my Ikea mirror, saying "Who the fuck are you? Why don't you just cut the crap and find out?"

There is a lull and nothing comes to me. That little rag doll on the advent calendar is glaring wickedly my way. I want to stick a pin through her eye. This shitty line of thinking sucks. I need to get on with the day. I quickly masturbate to a grainy video clip on my iPhone of a supposedly straight Middle-Eastern geek slobbering expertly over a really large disembodied cock.

Temporarily relieved, I dress for work, pulling together a really nice outfit to perk me up since I'm beginning to feel the impact of very little sleep. I also want to look pulled together because I'm making a pit stop on my way to work to visit Auntie Flora. I see her once a week. She's quite old and could quite possibly croak at any minute.

As I leave the house, I decide that today I will come up with ten things I want to do before I die. I am certain that constant anonymous sex is not going to be one of them.

AUNTIE FLORA IS a rambling old showgirl. My visits to her began a few months ago. She had a mild heart attack which triggered a desire to get to know her "only living relative." She's my dead father's baby sister and she's stinking rich. If she doesn't marry again (her husband, a mafia-connected Manhattan restaurateur, took a powder years ago) or if she doesn't lose her mind or come to hate the sight of me, I will inherit her somewhat dwindling fortune. Her most appealing asset is the grand two bedroom apartment she owns on Manhattan's elegant Upper West side, along with a shit load of original artwork including a Pollok and a Warhol.

She's a large, healthy-looking 80-year-old woman, with blue oval shaped eyes, glossy blonde hair and porcelain, precisely botoxed skin. She's still vibrant, though at times, between vast silences, her mind will spread open like a cobwebbed fan and blow out incoherent memories. I don't know if her tales are fact or fiction, most likely a mix. Her favorite subjects are a six year period when she made summer visits to my parent's farm in Arkansas when I was child, and her brief time on the New York stage. I remember she'd come every summer when I was six up until I was twelve. Then the visits stopped, though I don't recall why.

Auntie Flora's grand theatrical career (Florence Tanner on a marquis) burned electrically in the early part of the 1960s, then went abruptly black once she married. I am pretty certain she chose to quit the stage. She's a tough broad, so I can't see her being bullied by anyone, even a mafia-connected brute of a husband. Truth is, her husband, who boxed before he bought swanky eateries, looks pretty steaming hot in the photos I've seen. I'd fuck him.

I've biked to her apartment this morning and am watching her now. Auntie Flora is seated in a throne-like chair in her living room, her head bowed in a short nap. I believe that, at heart, Flora is a tough backwoods Arkansas woman who faced wave after wave of brutal poverty and cruelty growing up, just like my father. Her harsh, warrior instincts are hidden under layers of expensive clothing, refined speech patterns and cash, but like an insect with a secret stinger, she strikes when threatened. She's snoring lightly.

I say little during our visits, mostly because I'm afraid of offending her and losing the promised inheritance, but when she does speak, I feel like a secretary hired to jot her memoirs. Today, we've been sitting for fifteen minutes in silence. She is lifting her head, but her eyes remain shut. She licks her lips, like a tired cat.

Propped up like a doll on a fainting couch near her, I glance around the room and imagine rearranging the antique living room furniture for a chic little orgy. We face a bank of tall windows looking out onto West End Avenue. It's always like this, the set up, and there is always a plate of ginger snap cookies on a small table dividing us. Neither of us touches the snaps. I imagine we are both watching our waist lines.

"I want to show you something," she says snapping her eyes open, suddenly awake.

She reaches for one of her many photo albums. I have to admit that I am oddly comforted by these bland little visits. So little is expected of me and I honestly believe that at times she forgets who

I am. It all feels slightly anonymous which I like. It's also nice to spend time with someone I have no intention of screwing.

"Come sit here," she says, patting a Baroque, tassel-covered foot stool next to her.

She's opened the album to a black and white photo. On the left is a young Flora, quite striking in a floor length gown, her hair shellacked off her forehead and a huge diamond ring adorning one hand which is holding a champagne flute.

"That's the cunt," she says softly, pointing to the woman on the right.

I love when she cusses. She's pretty raw as that goes.

Smaller and curvier than Flora, the woman in the photo is darkly exotic with a mass of black hair, a silver screen smile and an incredible pair of breasts pushing aggressively forward in a white, form-fitting bead-encrusted, very low cut gown.

Flora, both now and in the photo, looks bitter and a little broken. There is more anger than grief in her eyes, but I imagine one is simply masking the other and I suddenly feel an intense and hurried connection between us that I really don't want to acknowledge. It's got to be time to go. I don't want to be too late for work.

"He took the picture, the fuck. He was doing her that very night," she says.

She snaps the album shut, which hopefully signals the end of this week's visit.

"I got them back," Flora says to button the memory, her eyes fluttering shut again.

Waiting for an exit signal from Flora, I momentarily try to recall exactly how her husband died and also think of my parent's double-headed funeral in Arkansas which Flora did not attend.

I had totally shut down through my parent's wake, sitting in their modest, ramshackle country home in a hard back chair, shaking the callused hands of men and women who work outside most of the year, listening to a mushy trail of unknown voices saying useless things.

The funeral was even worse. I refused to look at the coffin, and that's when the soft murmurs brushed around the place saying that I'd moved to the East Coast and gone a little crazy, which is really sort of true. The thing I remember most clearly is the boy I had sex with, later that night, on my parents front porch. He was the son of some neighbor and he'd been dragged to the funeral parlor like everybody in town, looking dumb and sloppy in overalls and a dirty cap, missing a tooth and built like a linebacker. It was almost campy, I thought, watching him shuffle through the line to tell me something that would mean absolutely nothing like: 'sorry for your loss' or 'they sure was some fine folks.' *Brutally stupid hicks, all of them*, I thought.

But that boy. He gave me something that day. At the cemetery, I wouldn't let go of his hand when we shook, because I remembered him from when I was in grade school. I remembered us doing things and I was in dire need of that sort of thing, to wipe the dark and dirty little funeral and my parent's abrupt departure out of my head. I asked him if he'd come by later to help me move a chifforobe, which is another name for an armoire. It was a blatant lie as I had no chifforobe. I stole the idea from the move *To Kill a Mockingbird* when the trashy white girl asks the local black man to bust up her chifforobe before she tries to molest him.

My backwoods boy, who was clearly gay, closeted, and desperate for touch, was easy to seduce. It was warm for November and the moon was full and I lapped on that boy's cock on my parent's porch so hard I choked, but I wouldn't let it out of my mouth. Because the pain, the gagging push down my throat, the salty taste of his fat cock and the stink of his boots smeared with country grass and cow dung so close, all that let me cry hard and loud and ragged and long. I cried harder than I ever have in my life. Crying like a man facing the electric chair or someone being gutted by a sadist serial killer. That stupid farm boy just kept fucking my face, with a mix of pity and remorse and a sideways glance that said he knew I was grieving in my

Diary of a Sex Addict

own fucked up way.

Flora is lolling her head forward, and I wonder if she might actually topple out of her chair. She opens then closes her big blue eyes, nods her head, and raises one hand in a ritualistic gesture which indicates I should show myself out. She does this every week when she's had enough. I wonder if she's dreaming.

As I go, I also wonder if I could copy her pose and use it to let tiresome sex tricks know it's time to get the hell out. The door snaps shut, and Flora and the past, dissolve, as I head downtown to work.

THERE'S A TERRIFYING disconnect at my job, which I brush quickly away and call boredom. Because anything more real would be so uncomfortable that I'd need a cock in every hole. I work at a domestic violence shelter. This terrible disconnect I feel is three-fold, similar I realize to my triple-threat nightly sex hunt. No deeper meaning with this, just coincidence—though a fortune teller once told me that three is my lucky number.

On one level, the female clients who come to see their counselors are smiling—Patty and Gert or Emma who is very young and on the antipsychotic drug Zyprexa. I hear them laugh and talk about shopping. One woman, Suzy, sings loudly and off key. She is blind and taps her cane with the rhythm. Her abuser threw acid in her face and eyes.

This leads me to level two, which is the fact that while they sing and chit chat, I enter their caseworker's notes, compiled from raggedy notebooks, into a computer. I type things like *abuser blinded Suzy, abuser raped then locked Raven in a closet for two days*. This transcribing job, this list of horrors disconnecting me from the laughter of the women, is the shelter's feeble attempt to get modern. It's also why I have a job. In the two years I've been here, however, they have used me for a host of things beyond typing. My expertise covers everything from party planning to cleaning the refrigerator. For job security, I've also started typing the progress notes more slowly.

Level three of the boredom-disconnect, is, well, it's me. To deal with this boredom or horror, or whatever it is, at least once a day I walk through the room where one of the female empowerment groups is meeting. I lock myself in the little bathroom, disrobe and take pictures of myself erect in different muscle poses that I then post on Grindr to lure an afternoon hookup. I don't think about anything when I take these pictures, and I don't really listen to the women's soft voices coming through the door talking about self-esteem and self-love.

I just take my pictures then flush the toilet and go back to my desk.

Today, with four new sexy pictures loaded from my iPhone to Grindr, I already have two hook-up choices. One is a mere five blocks away, which could be accomplished in the time allotted for a long coffee break. I only use a full lunch hour if it's something really special, like a college kid who wants to dress up in football gear and get fucked while his lover watches. That level of heat.

The women's self-esteem group is letting out. I hover over my computer and type to look busy, grumpy, and unavailable, indicating that I have one of my (fake) migraines. A migraine history can account for all sorts of sick days. Nobody can really prove you don't have a migraine and most people are baffled and freaked out by the concept, as if they could catch it or something. My Granny had migraines when she ate chocolate so I feel it's quasi-real. I'm co-opting her awful pain that nobody ever noticed and she never complained about.

This line of thinking, this random fakeness, is how I justify a lot of my behavior. As Blind Suzy taps by with her cane, I'm typing one of her old case notes into the new modern system. I'm embarrassed, entering intimate details as she blindly rattles by singing a Tina Turner song.

The suicide episode was a fantasy. Note to Dr. Caldell. Client's meds need attention. While she has not suffered abuse for six years, since the blinding and the nail gun wounds, client's fantasizes that she is being followed by her abuser. Note to…'

I can only type these raw little life turds in short spurts. The group of ladies has dispersed and the case managers have retreated to their offices to spritz water on dying plants and make endless phone calls. I'm alone at my desk.

I text my reclusive friend Michael the painter who has vowed to lose ten pounds before leaving the house this month.

what up

I wait. The iPhone screen dulls and there is that slagging slump into emptiness. Michael is my only non-sexual friend. We met one wet Sunday afternoon last summer, both of us aimlessly perusing the LGBT "Group Meeting" board for something to do. We bonded over our disdain for titles like "Gay Senior Scuba Diving" and "Bi Bridge Club" and later over fucked-up personal issues we both chose to keep purposely vague.

He texts.

fat fat fat. watching oprah. I am a whale. lady orca. harpoon me now.

When he gets on his 'I hate my fat self' binges there's nothing to do. I secretly enjoy occasional food gorging as a way to numb out, but I learned not to mention this to him. Once I told Michael my real lover was pizza maker Papa John. He was deeply offended. I'm not in the mood today to cheer him up so I text back.

ur fine. boss just came in.

I get on Grindr and find someone pretty quickly. He calls himself 'F'. He has a big cock in a tiny profile picture. He says he's a hairdresser in a salon nearby.

cum over he texts, *i work near you*

My fantasy wilts as I envision a middle-aged man with chunky blonde streaks who loves the *Golden Girls* and wants to be fucked with the handle of a blow dryer.

In the pause, F sends a new text: *I'm nine inches.*

I put my 'gone on coffee break' sign up, turn off my computer and head out.

Michael texts me:

am I a sad sack
I reply.
never. can't talk. work got busy.
Sometimes it's best to tell people what they wish to hear.

THE PLACE SMELLS like bleach. Though I imagine hair bleach is different from getting-the-sheets white Clorox bleach, the scent takes me for a split second to my mother, doing laundry on a hot summer day, lugging those heavy damp sheets from the washer to our clothes line in the back yard. I used to lie on the lawn and watch her hoisting yards of wet cotton, looking all sturdy and determined, both fierce and sad.

I'm not really off to a sexy start.

I think his name is Claude, not 'F' which is what he told me on Grindr. 'Claude's' is stenciled on the door of this chic little East Village hair salon. He said that he owned the place in his final text, so I step in and say "Hi Claude" and he looks at me like I just shoved a steak knife up his ass.

I wonder if I should have said 'Yo fuckah' since there are no clients. That's when the tiny dog starts yapping. I'm several feet away but I think Claude is sweating. His mouth is tight in anger and he reels on the dog, an Italian Miniature Greyhound I think. With his back to me Claude grabs the dog off of the ground by the collar and literally throws him into a back room.

This actually turns me on, this man-handling of the dog. Claude may have promise as a total asshole capable of really mean, hot, mindless sex. I begin to get aroused. As Claude draws close I notice a line of tiny ant tattoos crawling up his right arm. Behind him, two huge photos of a 1970s Jane Fonda hang on the wall near three chrome hair dryers and a really nice high-tech black sink with a funky looking pink hose.

Claude comes straight up to me and puts his hands on my chest and smiles. His teeth are grey which is an absolute turn-

Diary of a Sex Addict

off. If I'm going to give this a thumbs down, I have to do it now. I can mutter, "not a match man", or "sorry dude" or something. But as is very often the case, I feel myself slipping toward an irritating depression thinking this was a waste of time and how can I get through the work day and another awful women's group without getting off? So I roughly grab his crotch and feel his erection and it's large. I shut my eyes and go to kiss him but he's turned his head so I kiss air, and taste bleach. The dog is yapping loudly.

Claude steps away to turn up the music, Kelly Clarkson, who I like but not for sex. He takes his pants and underwear off and waves me over. I get on my knees, but am a few feet away, so have to awkwardly crawl to his cock, realizing he has a silver ring piercing the skin below his head which makes me gag. But again, I'm so far into it I shut my eyes and start to suck this thing, and very, very quickly, as the dog yaps louder, I jack myself off to orgasm.

I've become pretty good at the super quick jack off, for collapsing cases like this. The orgasm momentarily softens the sting of a dreary hook-up.

Claude has barely begun his pleasure build. He steps back, frowning in disbelief, staring at my pool of cum on the shiny tile floor. The dog keeps barking.

"Why didn't you give me a heads up you were ready, dude?"

I stand and zip up and turn away, thinking Claude is too old to use the term dude.

"It's been a really long time. Sorry. You're hot man," I say with as much enthusiasm as I can muster, which is little.

I don't turn back, just move swiftly toward the salon's front door as Claude screams brutal threats at the dog. As I shut the door behind me, I hear the sound of a fist slapping dog ass. Walking back to work, I imagine myself fucking a Great Dane with wild abandon. I find this too kinky even for me.

Back at my desk, I block Claude's profile on my Grindr account.

december 10

MY PARENTS HAVE both been dead for over ten years. I have no siblings. I don't miss them, honestly. I used to think of my parents like a rainstorm, uncertain yet regular, something that will come and go, both irritating, and before sleep, soothing. I don't know why they appear to me in the shape of a rainstorm, but that's how I feel.

I used to visit them, on their farm in Arkansas, every summer. I never went for Christmas. The holiday flight was expensive, I said. They never argued.

They seemed very content to me. When I fantasize about the accident, which happened close to Thanksgiving, I see the two of them in my father's cherry red pickup truck and I imagine them happy and sitting close, driving at night on a wet, winding rural road. Swift and elegant, that death. I think it's pretty normal to think of them as Christmas approaches, but I don't like to dwell on it. I suppose my visits to Auntie Flora have stirred the memories about a bit. I hang a small felt elf's face on my mother's advent calendar and sit on the floor of my kitchenette. The elf can keep that bitchy little rag doll ornament company.

What will get me away from all this useless memory crap is the plotting of the weekend sex binge. Work today was long, slow and drab. I got through it by imagining about what type of sex fiends I would lure into my lap.

I perch now on the edge of the weekend binge, and the image that keeps flashing in my mind is not the college wrestler stud I fantasized about at lunch, but me squatting near a giant cage. I see myself in the cage swinging on a happy little bar, like Tweetie Bird in a Warner Bros. cartoon. My last big weekend binge was months ago and ended with a skinny street kid pulling a knife on me and stealing my wallet and a pair of Gucci loafers. But that won't happen this time. It will be hot and happy. It's Christmas and I deserve this.

I have eaten very little white flour in the past week so my tummy is flat and I look refreshed. This morning I shot a bunch of pictures in my super-small 2Xist underwear with the push-out pouch. My cock looks so much bigger than it really is in the shots and I don't give a shit if it's an illusion. With a binge, the point is to get the men in the house. Once they enter they rarely run away.

I caught nine good images of myself including three with a boner popping up over the top of the blue-grey striped waist band. Once I post the pics on Grindr and Manhunt and get the porn running on my DVD player, I can hop on the phone line and begin my triple play. I feel like Caligula, not during his crazy years, more the fawn-like over-sexed boy Emperor.

I settle in for a disco nap. Nothing really starts happening until after midnight.

december 11

HE'S SEXY IN dim light.

Speedoboy is clearly not a boy, but I'm guessing not far from forty and incredibly lean to the point of being bony. Never too rich, too thin, too hung. His Speedo is royal blue and very tight. He smiles a lot, though I wish he wouldn't because he could use a good orthodontist.

I fall back on my sofa. Speedoboy comes at me like he's going to dive, then he lands with his torpedo thin body on top of me. He grinds our crotches together. His cock is big and if he weren't so rough and anxious it would feel good. He's resting his long skinny arms on the back of the sofa getting louder with his "Oh fuck yes baby" calls when a single drop of blood lands on my shoulder. I think of the saint that cried blood tears, St. Agnes. I was raised Catholic and recall an art project making cardboard cut-outs of every saint born in the month of December.

Speedoboy has leapt up and is now lying on the floor. He's very quiet. His fingers squeeze his tiny nose.

"It will stop," he says.

I've never known anyone who has suffered nose bleeds so I just sit and wait, wishing he would say something. In the silence, the porno plays softly like background music at a party. A Yugoslavian wrestler is having a serious talk with a student wrestler. There are subtitles. It's awkward that no one is having sex. The porn actors are discussing something and my sex date is breathing deeply and clutching his nose. This is not how I imagined kicking off my weekend binge. At once the two wrestlers stop talking and shove tongues in mouths and Speedoboy hops up and shouts.

"I'm good."

I stand and go to the kitchenette to get water.

"Are you all right?" he says, confused, as if I am the one who just spontaneously bled all over the fucking place.

"I need a break," I say with as little emotion as possible.

Speedoboy looks crestfallen. His shoulders slope as he dresses. He slowly leaves, fingering the edge of his nostrils.

I'M STUCK IN the middle of a dull patch. There are three men on Grindr that are 'on their way' which means nothing. More than half of the men 'on their way' dissolve and disappear. Often their tiny Grindr pictures vanish too. I sometimes wonder if they ever really existed. Was 'Latino8' really coming by or did I drift off and dream that one?

I actually had a stray text from my friend Michael.

seven more pounds and ill be fit to be seen.

I would like to reply, but can't risk his wanting to fire up a full-fledged text discussion. That would be too distracting. I'll touch base later. I hang a faded candy cane on the advent calendar, next to the elf face.

I've lost track of time. There was one reject after Speedoboy. He was nameless, from the phone line, promising all sorts of muscle and hunky love. At the door, wearing a baseball cap and leather jacket, he had the lost look of an elderly drunk who just had a stroke. His hands shook. His eyes were bleary but a pretty blue. I wanted to hug him and guide him to a hospital but I said "Not a match," and quickly shut the door listening to his muffled sighs and footsteps drifting slowly back down the four flights.

My three 'on the way' Grindr men are slow and my lids are heavy. My door buzzes. I have no idea who it is but I buzz him up hoping for the best.

He calls himself 'TantricZ'. He's sort of attractive with wavy red hair and a face like a worn-out Harrison Ford. He's a little chunky but well dressed.

"I only want to play with you. You don't need to touch me. Let me honor and worship your cock," he says.

I find this mildly appealing though I realize he's not any of my three 'on the way' Grindr men. He may be from the phone line, or anywhere really. I give my address out indiscriminately. I lie back. He begins to touch me gently like a secret massage fairy who has crept out of the wall. I feel taken care of. There's a pause and I smell the stink of poppers. He's sucking on the little bottle of amyl nitrate, an over the counter gay party drug that is akin to sniffing paint fumes or gasoline.

"I am your slave," he whispers.

He's attaching something to the head of my penis and the massage fairy swiftly transforms into a serial killer maniac. I sit up to see a tiny purple rubber circle on my cock. The rubber is attached by a thin wire to a tiny pink box. He switches it on and I am being tickled and massaged. It feels like little fingers so I lie back, but with hesitation, because this little thing is electric and he's snorting poppers again. He's mumbling something, which I begin to imagine is another language, the tantric sex slave tongue. Between the slurping of the popper bottle up his flaring nostrils and the guttural mumbling, he is rapidly losing any scrap of appeal, piercing the tenuous fantasy bubble that keeps these slutty sessions afloat. This scent of the mundane is ruinous. I am quickly sinking to a dark place I usually only find alone in the tub. My black hole.

There is nothing worse than being in the midst of a mildly amusing sex binge and falling into my black hole. With my eyes shut, this tingling pink thing on my penis head, and my sex slave pushing out popper scented breaths, I can more and more clearly see the edge of my black hole. I'm feeling this awful weight in my face. I suppose most people would call this being on the brink of tears, but that's not my experience. Tears are nowhere near. It's just a heaviness slowly surrounding my head. Everything in the room feels incredibly close and tight and there is this invisible suffocating scarf folding gently around my throat.

My mouth is tight, my eyes throb. The hollow of my cheeks feel full, as if I sucked in a breath underwater and took in magical airy water that is somehow getting thick and hard. Of course, there is no water, no scarf. It's all empty even my cheeks and face so I force open my eyes and confront the TantricZ-man to try to get things back on a sexy track.

He's looking very closely at me. His face soft and loose, like a wave, like he's in the hole with me, as he tilts his head to one side.

"You are the saddest man I have ever seen," he says.

Then he gathers his things, gently pulls the pink contraption off of my penis, puts away his poppers and leaves.

Things have got to get better.

I'M LEANING INTO the door, naked, stroking my penis to keep it hard with one hand and holding the peep-hole knob up with another. I cannot take another dreary man, or an old man, or a tantric slave who tells me I'm sad. If this fellow does not look promising, then I'm ditching the binge, ordering a fatty Papa

John's Meat Lovers pizza and watching cartoons.

He's from Grindr and calls himself 'Jocko.' Through the peep-hole he's adorable, young, masculine and clearly a little desperate. I am studying his tiny face through the hole as he stares unwittingly ahead. This peep view is very similar to the tiny shots on Grindr. As he tentatively steps in I decide that you can determine a lot about someone through miniscule visuals.

Jocko is carrying a large duffle bag. He does not look at me, which is a relief after TantricZ. He strides in, sets down his bag and begins to undress. We are silent. He's very orderly, folding his sweat pants, socks and shirt on the floor by his bag. I imagine he's in his mid-20s, and works out a lot. He is incredibly lean, with a ripple of muscle in his stomach. His hair is buzzed short.

Once un-draped, he stares at me a little too long. And for a very brief second, he is a reflection of me, that dead emptiness in his eyes, that searching desperation. Luckily he rubs his hand along his tight belly toward his crotch and I completely forget myself, which is the point. The jock strap he wears is ratty and colored shades of gray, white and yellow. It is loose and old and stained with what looks like years of piss, cum and spit. His cock is bobbing inside of it quite impressively, and he's rubbing the whole package.

He nods down, and I presume he wants me to go there. So I do. It smells horrible, which disgusts and excites and challenges me. He moans ever so softly, revealing his obvious fetish for stench, so I open my mouth wide and suck on that stinky jock thing. I suck on it and make it wet, I gobble at the strap edges, I try to suck years of old gunk out of it. All the while he is moaning and I am happy to finally find something hot and lewd. The more I suck, the more awful it tastes and smells. But the further away my black hole dissipates. I am nothing but the grossness of this jock and his lean young hands on my head pushing me back and forth. I love the vileness of this thing in my mouth. It's absolutely liberating. I want this to go on and on, and it does for quite awhile.

Then he abruptly pushes me away and motions to the wide-open sofa bed. I lie down on it. He's fishing inside his duffle, and I have my typical 'could there be a chainsaw in there' *American Psycho* moment. But I become intrigued as he pulls out six different jock straps and three sport cups.

I am not athletic, and have never even seen a cup. In fantasy, I have imagined hockey players or football studs shoving them over huge cock baskets. He comes at me quickly now, all hesitation and gentleness gone, as he puts a white hard athletic cup over my face. I think of that oxygen mask that drops from the hatch above you on a crashing airplane, and also of a Ken doll's curved smooth plastic genitals. The cup fits nicely over my nose and mouth and smells funky, but nothing like his putrid jock. He begins to play with my cock, as he holds the cup on my mouth. He is grunting and I imagine he's happy. I'm enjoying the multiple sensations, the musky smell of the cup, his hands on me.

I would like to kiss him, but he seems very much in control now, so I dare not be too bold. He removes the cup and replaces it with another, this one sheathed inside an 'armor gear' jock strap which seems larger than the usual type, maybe for super well-endowed rugby players. He's pushing it roughly onto my face and it's pressing uncomfortably into my cheek but I don't want to complain because I never want him to leave. I shut my eyes and let him push the cup harder and harder into my face and I try to suck deeper because I think he would like this. I inhale steadily and think of the novel I snuck into my parent's barn and read, *The Story of O*. I also think of the S&M film *Nine & A Half Weeks* starring Kim Bassinger and a pre face-lifted Mickey Rourke. Sucking on the cup, I decide that all of these characters shared a deep love.

I hope Jocko stays for a full day or two and overwhelms my life. The cup has cut into my cheek, and tiny drops of blood creep up out of my skin, which flashes me uncomfortably back to the earlier nosebleed with Speedoboy. Blood trickles onto the cup's white plastic. It is obviously a wildly erotic trigger for

Jocko because he immediately climaxes, shooting his cum on my belly without uttering a sound. He pulls the cup away, examining it like a precious jewel, wiping away all traces of blood with another jock strap. Then he dresses, packs his duffle and never looking at me, quickly exits.

I lie there, sad yet content, realizing that nobody ever really says goodbye properly.

december 12

THE WEEKEND BINGE has been, other than Jocko, mostly a flop. To avoid a long sink into my black hole, I am dead set on a slutty finale which should exhaust me and lead me back into the work week.

His name is Pig. The straightforwardness of his tag intrigues me. He says he wants me to slap him a little and spit on him. I have never done this sort of thing but I think it will be pretty easy. I tell Pig to come in two hours. To fortify, since I've eaten very little for days, I order a Papa John's pizza and hang a snowflake on the advent calendar.

I put on a robe, then loosen it a little at the last second to intrigue the delivery boy. He's Mexican and notices my barely hidden nudity, but seems to be in an incredible hurry. Everyone, it seems, is in a rush these days.

As I eat in the dark, I think of forgetting the sex and binge eating. I could cancel Pig, or just not answer the buzzer when he snorts at the door. I briefly consider running out for a five-pound box of Cheez-Its, an Entenmann's Deluxe French cheesecake and a carton of Ben & Jerry's Chubby Hubby ice cream. This idea swiftly dies as I load up some incredibly nasty free porn on the internet and wait for my lovely little piglet.

He's from the phone line and his description was vague so I can envision him anyway I wish. I lie on the floor, anticipating something wonderful and insane. My apartment's radiator poles are hissing, like a kitty trapped in the wall. I am feeling more and more childlike, waiting for Pig. Maybe it's his farm animal name, giving rise to a *Charlotte's Web* memory, or it could be the food settling me down or my lack of sleep finally tilting me toward illusion.

The place is getting very hot which I like. The hissing is both cat and snake now. I hear a distant voice, the neighbor couple, and I realize I have missed them. They must have gone away for the weekend because things have been very quiet. Her voice rings high in laughter. I'm starting to sweat and allow myself to drift to sleep for just a moment.

I WAKE IN pitch black, still lying on the hard floor. There is no hissing. My iPhone glows. Pig was due hours ago. I text him:

whats up

He sends an immediate reply:

at party. can come now

I hesitate, wondering if this dullish binge has already secretly finished while I slept, if the food capped it, and if in this bleak darkness I can crawl to the sofa bed and sleep peacefully until the next day's work.

you can cum on my tongue his text glows.

Pig's gnarly text convinces me there's one last breath in my binge so I send him the address and wait. I won't let him touch me. If he lets men cum on his tongue, then he's not safe and who knows what he's about. A sane man would reject him outright, but I lay no claims on sanity. After all, I just had a pink electrical gadget placed on my penis.

I will do very little with Pig. It will not be a finale. It will be a brief epilogue until my next big adventure. The buzzer sounds. I stand at the door and don't even touch the peep-hole. I swing open the door and stand in the empty hall nude, waiting anxiously for my Pig. Coming up the last flight he glares at me, puffing and sweaty and I recall a children's book where the swine huffs and puffs and blows someone's house down.

His face is attractive but I doubt his claim of being twenty-eight due to the feathered gray hair at his temples. But if he weren't stocky he would be quite attractive. Pig comes in, a bit sheepishly, grinning.

I AM A very angry man, which is why Pig says he loves me.

On his knees, on my JC Penney tanglewood blue floral rug, he is dressed. He remains dressed the whole time. His fetish is about something else.

I reel back and slap him hard, take a deep breath, then spit on his face. My spittle globs on his shiny cheek and I think he looks pretty, like a happy boy at a Christmas feast with a touch of sweet globby pastry dough mixed with rain on his face. Pig makes me think of all sorts of bizarre things, and nothing is adding up. He shuts his eyes and leans his head back in expectation. I slap the other side of his face, but have no spittle left. He lies his mouth in my lap.

"Suck it nasty pig," I say.

He's reeling with this, and I know I have to start to hit him again. He can't go too long without some sort of mean touch, and I decide this is an unexpectedly good finale after all. I smack him in the head and there is a weird popping sound. I don't care if I just gave him a brain tumor, or jarred him so he flies into a coma or becomes lobotomized. The feeling of my hand on his hard head feels good and he keeps moaning and pleading so I keep hitting him. I spit again. Then I grab his hair and yank his face back.

"You nasty fucker, squeal Piglet."

Of course he does, falling back on my tanglewood rug and squealing and I wonder if the cute little neighbor couple think I bought a pot belly pet pig for Christmas. The landlord allows no pets.

He sticks out his tongue still snorting and heaving, and he suddenly is quite disgusting to look at with his matted hair and a slight bruise on his ear and all that sweat. Determined to finish, I work myself up quickly and deliver onto his tongue. Pig lies with his mouth open, his tongue lolling out now stained with the white glob of my cum. He keeps his mouth open, and I imagine he is in a fairy tale, a frog or prince waiting for a kiss to turn into something other than a fat man sweating on my floor. I stand and stretch then go to get water. I do not turn around, just listen to the noises of Pig as he sighs, moans, mutters and dresses. I do not turn from the sink but stand still waiting, hoping he will simply vanish.

He does. The door whispers open then shut. I know I will never see him again.

december 13

THE PIG CONNECTION has left me irritable and moody. The morning is gray and ugly and I feel like an utter failure in life, for the moment at least. I don't want sex immediately, so I decide to stop and see Auntie Flora before work. I need a distraction, something soothing, maybe even a ginger snap before I face the day.

My bike ride across town invigorates me, and I'm glad I decided to kick start my day this way. I park out front and head up, feeling worlds better. In the elevator, my stomach lurches from a lack of food, and I have a brief and unexpected feeling of doom.

The door to Auntie Flora's home is ajar, which is bizarre. It's always locked and I let myself in. She gave me a key to the place after a few visits which I thought was risky on her part. Then again she knows nothing about me really, so wouldn't guess that I may sneak in some day and fuck a drugged-up trick on her Mahogany dining room table.

I move in swiftly, ignoring my instinct that says turn back, sure there will be a logical explanation. I breath easier as I step in and spot her life-long assistant, Lottie, cradling a cell phone in the living room. Lottie is a bit of a behemoth. There is no space between her thick head and her wide shoulders and her body is very square. Her hair is long, straight and dishwater brown and she wears cheap, ugly clothing and white nurse's shoes. We've met a few times. Her most striking characteristic is her snort. To punctuate even the dullest sentence, she scrunches her fat head into her troll-like shoulders and lets rip a fit of deep nasal laughter. She's usually not around during my visits.

She sees me, holds the phone away, and looks about to speak but stops and pauses. Then she shakes her big head vigorously and waves me toward Auntie's bedroom.

"Go," she says. "Your sister's waiting."

Snort.

We've never officially been introduced, but I'm a bit shocked that she thinks Flora is my sibling. I head down a hall, past the arched entry of a big, vacant kitchen toward the bedroom. I always visit Auntie Flora in the living room. I've never even seen her bedroom. The pictures lining the hall are of my family. My mother and father looking extremely young and happy on a tractor. Mom is wearing short-shorts and a checkered, collared top tied at the waist. Her hair is piled on her head and her lips are full. She's beautiful. My father sits next to her on the metal machine, miles of field behind him, his arm draped across her shoulder, a wide grin, shirtless and lean, dungarees and a half smoked cigarette dangling. They look amazing and I feel I have never met these people. The parent's I knew are flat wax replicas in my memory. Their lives were full of passionless, satisfied routine.

The next image is of my father and myself. I'm puny, probably three, wearing an adorable ensemble of tan shorts, a white short sleeve shirt and a polka dot bow tie. I'm barefoot and standing on my tiptoes, clutching my father's hand and grinning. My father is in a brown wool suit. I have no memory of this day, this picture. I don't ever remember being that joyous. I wonder if it's actually a neighbor who looks like me.

A long and drawn out moan seeps from under the shut bedroom door. Could Flora being getting laid in there? An elderly gentlemen caller doing his thing, or a young gigolo hired by Lottie to spice things up? I make my way toward the moan hoping for the latter.

No such luck.

The bedroom is straight out of Dickens. I imagine the archaic four-poster bed, the pair of velvet chairs, the big marble vanity table could all net me a good deal of cash at a Sotheby's auction after Auntie's death.

Flora is buried under a mound of quilts. There is a big china pitcher near her. Her head is propped up nicely but her hair, normally yanked back tight and neat, is hanging limply around her shoulders. I am aware it could be a wig. Her eyes are vacant.

I want to turn heel and flee, but I step closer out of fear of offending her.

"Regret," she says.

Her eyes fly open and she sits up very straight as if suddenly possessed.

"Benny you wicked thing come here," she says, staring straight at me and patting the side of her bed.

I have no idea who Benny is, but I do as I'm told, curious as to what this old woman may have up her obviously delusional sleeve. I scan the bedside table for drugs (there are six white pill bottles and one long tube of liquid). She takes my hand.

"What do you regret the most," she says. "I mean what do you hate even remembering, so much that you can't stand that it ever happened?"

I'm not Benny, and I can't tell if she recognizes me or is in a drug-induced dream state, so I do not answer. I feel stuck at her side and as she breathes heavily, clutching my hand, I can't help but answer her question in my head. I am suddenly propelled by this strange old woman to revisit a very bad memory. I wish I'd simply gone to work.

It was a sexual scene several years ago that, for most people, may have really curbed their exploits. I, of course, am not most people when it comes to lurid sex. This thing that happened though, I wish I could erase it. Afterwards, I was turned off to sex for nearly two weeks.

It was back when I was only using the phone line to hookup. I hadn't yet discovered Grindr or Manhunt and mostly had sex on weekends, not during the week. My daily dependence didn't really kick in until after the break-up of my relationship with my ex-lover Ben.

It was summer. I'd been to the public pool on Manhattan's East Side. It's smaller than most of the city's Olympic-sized pools which are jammed with screeching kids. It's frequented mostly by young Latinos. There'd been a small gang of teen gangster boys. A kid with a shaved head and a tight little body looked familiar. He'd fondled himself and winked at me.

I had no idea if he was ready to get secretly blown, or wanted to blow my faggot head off, so I left. The scene got me going, though, so later that evening, I cruised the phone line and got invited to what a man with a raspy voice described as a very wild group scene in a Midtown loft.

Flora is snoring softly now, but her grip on my hand is solid. I try to unhook, but my slightest movement causes her to grip more tightly. I shut my eyes, returning to my own scene of past sexual regret.

The mid-town loft with the promised orgy was in a gray and nondescript building. A groggy, wrinkled doorman called upstairs to clear me, then unlocked an elevator to the fifth floor and sent me up. The doors opened into a big dark and empty room. There were several plastic drop cloths on the floor and a half dozen naked men lounging. They were all young, which surprised me. There was a cloud of smoke hovering above but I

Diary of a Sex Addict 39

didn't see crack pipes or even cigarettes. It was a silent place. A chunky-muscled, dark skinned guy came right up to me and kissed, then started to undress me. I was ready to cum right away, having been so turned on at the pool earlier that day, and now stepping into what seemed to be a horny youth camp.

It turned ugly quickly.

Flora is still snoring lightly, and I really want to go. I need to get out, to get away from this old woman and her hallway relic photos and these irksome memories of bad, bad sex that have crept out of my head. Where's Floras story of regret? The old bitch brought it up. Why isn't she telling me a story to get me out of myself?

As I finally pry my hand away and stand to go, I am assaulted by a grainy image of that night in the midtown loft, and of a vision of a boy who lost his ear.

The chunky-dark guy that kissed me in the loft lead me to a circle of nude men on a big sheet of plastic. They were surrounding a kid who looked high-school age. There was a needle dangling from his arm, as if it had been left there by an errant nurse, and there were clamps on his nipples and on his nut sack which was rapidly turning purple like a rancid little prune. One of the men began to shove a large black dildo up the kid's ass. The kid didn't move and I was terrified, thinking he could be dead, knowing this was not the kind of scene I could handle. The chunky guy was biting my neck, then someone else was at my ear.

"We gonna fuck the little bitch up, we gonna fuck the bitch so bad yeah yeah yeah like da devil."

It seemed that they'd already been working on this boy for awhile, and I knew I had to get away but before I could, a tall skinny man with a skinny dangling cock and an old-school razor bent down and expertly sliced off half of that child's ear. Blood was shooting out in wide arcs and men were moaning and I swear someone was singing as I ran.

Now, I shut the door quietly on the sleeping Flora and make my way quickly out, unable to forget the most horrendous detail of that day. The entire trip down in the elevator, away from that brief but horrible little scene, I had a hard on.

That is a memory I will continually try to destroy. I suddenly hate Auntie Flora, big fat inheritance or not. She's clearly some sort of witch. I'm actually happy to be going to my drab little job. My own memories, I think, are sometimes worse than the brutal case notes I have to type up.

A LONG, GRAY work day. I quickly shelve away the Flora visit, type case notes and zone out.

No sex offers come. Nobody replies to any of my taunts on Grindr or Manhunt. Michael is not returning my texts, which means he has likely gained some weight and is busy spiraling into his own fat-fueled black hole. I trudge through the beginning of the work week only half alive, and make it home and into bed early. I hang a religious looking star on the advent calendar, then find comfort in *Family Guy* cartoons and a pan of gooey oven-baked Pillsbury cinnamon buns. All that fatty dough sinks into my belly and I welcome sleep.

december 14

IT'S 4 A.M.

I wake, groggy and reach for my iPhone which I keep near me like a security teddy bear on my bed. Half asleep, dreamless, I log into Grindr. I get these urges after a dull sex-void day at work. Suddenly near dawn I have to find out what's going on, what I may have missed, if anyone sent me a message asking to get fucked.

On Grindr, I notice a man in an elegant thumbnail picture with a miniscule swan near him. It disturbs me. I'm more fully awake now. I sit up properly and register the tiny picture on the Grindr profile page. The man himself has a long elegant neck and he is out of doors, looking over a precipice. I mostly notice the tiny swan in the picture's background floating on a green lake. It's all postage stamp sized, but it's very clearly shot and looks like it was taken on holiday. I imagine the man is searching for something. His Grindr text, typically relaying the size of the cock or sexual preference, simply says: *photographs. no strings. pro.*

I log in, feeling giddy and weirdly wonderland-like. He's actually online. The Swan Man is online at 4 A.M. So I text.

Hey.

I wait as the screen dims a little, then more and finally fades out to sleep. I'm left in the pitch black, thinking of getting up, or dialing the phone line, or trying to sleep a few more hours until the alarm goes off.

Grindr makes this odd gurgling noise when you receive a text. Almost like a sea bass burping under water. I'm not sure how it does it. It's unlike any other sound I get on my iPhone. The underwater gurgle comes. It's Swan Man.

My heart jumps. I feel hopeful and happy. Everything's possible in this moment of a new text buddy, a new Grindr connection.

I wait before I read his text, prolonging this hopeful moment, knowing he may tell me to leave him alone. The fact is, I've been having text affairs lately, tangible, long dialogues sometimes for weeks. We talk, or rather we text, all the time and reveal layers of secrets like—*I'm scared of the dark* or *I like two tongues in my ass at once when I do poppers* or *I love spandex* or *I was adopted.*

The texts of course are not in that order. The more personal tid-bits pop in when I'm on a spree, usually really late at night like this. I'm pretty sure some of the men are on drugs. But still, I believe I could possibly, maybe, potentially, fall in love with one of them. Because wouldn't it mean they are as unhinged as me? My alter ego, my other half, could be out there alone on a pull-out sofa, texting sacred flecks of himself to a faceless someone in the dark. I long ago accepted that in dreams of romance. I am unabashedly juvenile.

The mystery, vagueness, and freedom of these texts allows me to slowly build a lover's image—his morals, brains, guts, heart, all through letters on a tiny iPhone screen. This creating of my text fuck-buddies has become fulfilling in a scary sort of way. When it's late at night like this and I can't sleep, I think that if I ever slip into my black hole the texts would follow me down, like a long trail of my own intestines that somehow became detached from my inner guts. With my texts I wouldn't be alone. The words of the text men would keep me company.

I'm ready. I open his text.

Hi he says.

I'm relieved.

I begin and the messages flow and we open slowly, touching just a little, then more aggressively, and pretty quickly we get close. He's visiting from Switzerland, he left home at 15, he's 23. He's a mix of Black and German. He's a photographer and wants to publish a coffee table book. He needs models.

I'm into it, I'm really into it. He wants some hot body shots. I indiscriminately fire questions, most which he answers: Would he take a few nude shots of me? Would he watch me jack off? Would he eat dinner with me after? What sign is he? Where did the tiny Swan picture come from?

Nearly an hour later, I'm way over my monthly iPhone text limit but I don't care. I feel happy as dawn hits. I have a date. Photographs and cheesecake we've decided. It feels so fucking real.

The alarm is singing like a swan. I put an angel on the advent calendar.

I think I'm in love. Full of shit, but in love.

december 15

THE ABUSED WOMEN at work notice the difference in me. Patty guesses I have a date and the ladies swarm around after their 'Men and Violence' support group. Blind Suzy starts to sing a Tina Turner song and they all want details. These women know men and can sniff out romance. They've all had oodles of relationships. Most of them violent and horrible, but still relationships. I have not. I open up a little and tell them I want to make a cheesecake, but am freaked out so I'm buying one.

They coo and paw at me, and start shouting out advice, and Blind Suzy sings 'What's Love Got To Do With It' until one of the caseworkers emerges from spritzing her plants in her office and shoos the group away from my desk.

I pickup an Entenmann's Deluxe French Style cheesecake and some Perrier and dust my studio. I hang a reindeer on the advent calendar then put on some really tight underwear hoping to make my ass look more bubbly than it really is. I wait for Swan Man to arrive. He's on time, but as I buzz him in I realize I have no idea what to do.

Normally, with a fuck date, we get right to it. I usually know in advance preferences like 'top', 'bottom', 'spandex lover'— important details like that. I suddenly feel ridiculous in my underwear and want to put clothes on but there's an aggressive and loud knock. So I just swing the door open and take a breath.

He comes in gasping from the four floor walk up. He's tall and reedy thin, and has a pretty face, looking almost Egyptian with brown-black skin, exotic wide eyes and nice lips. He's carrying all sorts of camera equipment and immediately sets up a laptop on the countertop I have in my kitchenette. He hasn't spoken yet or looked at me, and I have my typical 'well he could be an ax murderer' thought.

He's pulling out a camera and a tripod and moving deftly, lightly around the room. I think of the swan in his Grindr profile pic. He seems birdlike and elegant like a dancer and really in control of this whole thing. I am turned on by the fact that he doesn't seem to notice me and has taken over the place. I feel like a piece of furniture, like something pretty he's going to eventually get to and tilt in different directions and tell what to do.

As I wait, I unexpectedly think of another time, and a photograph, something I discarded long ago. He was an older boy and we were on a camp-out and he shot a big load of cum on my scrawny boy chest. Then he took a picture of me. He ordered me not to move, to stay still while he took these pictures on a little Kodak camera. I had never seen a boy shoot cum and when he did it, the twisting agony on his Irish freckled face and the grunts he made as the unexpected gunk spurt from his fat little cock absolutely petrified me. I hated lying there, waiting for him to finish taking those pictures, but when he did, I was at a loss for what to do. I didn't want to move or touch the nasty white jelly on my chest so I shut my eyes hoping it would sink into my skin and disappear. Eventually I looked up and he was gone. But there was a band of tough, snarling flies in the tent and one landed on my stomach in the glob, snuffing the stuff thirstily. I swear I saw in that black pinhead eye of that fly a fleeting terror. I was very tired, so I dressed and went home. The older boy moved away with his family to Minnesota at the end of the summer. I never saw him again and as time passed, I wondered if any of it really happened. I don't know what he did with my picture.

Swan Man stops swirling around with his equipment and pulls his long elegant black hands together and finally looks at me with those big Egyptian eyes.

"Can I have some water?" he asks.

"I have cheesecake," I say.

"Just water."

He lets me pass in the small kitchenette and I get him his water and watch him drink it very slowly. He even drinks his water in a controlled manner. That excites me.

"Can we move that mirror?" he asks.

This strikes a chord of terror in me. I hate moving things, as I think I will never get them back in the exact same right spot. It can drive me nuts. Plus, this is my Ikea mirror, where I study myself, where I shoot my personal pictures for Grindr and I wonder what this could mean that this Swan Man photographer wants to move my special mirror.

"I think we can use the wall as a background. It's really the only empty wall," he says.

Before I speak, he goes to the mirror and he lifts it and he moves it in front of the sink. I feel like I want to cry, to sort of crumble there so he can come and lift me up and kiss me and tell me everything. All the shit and horror I've put myself through, all the lost years and the horrible job and the bills and the big vat of emptiness, and of course my black hole—all of it, he will say, he understands. Then he will force his tongue into my silly little mouth.

None of that happens.

"Are these underwear okay?" I ask.

He nods and motions me to the wall. I stand, trembling while he adjusts a light and then without warning begins to shoot pictures. I feel dumb-struck, having no idea what I am supposed to do. It's like his camera is an extension of him, reaching out to slap me, hurling open its big ugly glass jaw and attacking every bone in me, every flaw and ugly bit of flesh. I want to cry again, then he speaks very softly.

"You are very hot," he says, again in that super-controlled tone. "Relax."

I sigh, feeling stupid, hopeless and juvenile, lacking any sense of control in my own home. And then I just start to cry, and my body jiggles and shakes, and I cover my face and I throw my head back and shut my eyes, pretty sure he will leave. He just keeps shooting and shooting and shooting. I'm aroused too while I cry, my cock looks pretty plump in my underwear.

Behind him is the Ikea mirror and I can see myself while he shoots pictures. I can see my chubby cock and I realize I need to hold my stomach in tighter. My chest looks awesome, my man-tits are perky, and my arms are solid. I see myself as another man, as some sexy creature in a big mirror looking at me and leering and saying "I'm so much fucking better than you and I would never have sex with you." I leer back and mouth "fuck you" to myself as Swan Man shoots.

"That's good," he says, falling to his knees and snapping some more.

I feel utterly insane, with my tears and my mirror image ridiculing me. I am really aroused because Swan Man is pretty damn cute and lean, and he's really focused and serious as he aims that thing at me, and flashes the lights, and just keeps going. I haven't had so much attention in a long time. Again I think of that freckled Irish kid in the tent, and I wonder if I really sort of liked the attention back then, and the fact that he for some bizarre reason wanted a picture of my naked little nine-year-old self.

The action stops.

"Why don't we try a few nudes? Can you lay on the floor, with the underwear around you ankles?" he says, turning away from me and filling his water glass in the sink.

I slowly push my underwear down and my cock pops forth all proud and shit. I feel free and happy as I lie on the floor, wanting this stranger to devour me with that camera, and in some way eliminate that memory in the tent. He is capturing me, my essence in that flashing box, and scrutinizing me like a sex trick never has, as if there is something important to look at, as if he is afraid to lose me if the bulb or this scene were to dissolve. This makes him perfect, in this moment at least, because he totally needs me.

He turns to me, rubs his chin and nods.

"That's good," he says. "Put one hand further down."

He indicates my crotch with his long elegant finger, covering his own crotch as he nods to me.

I put my hand there.

"Why don't you take off your pants?" I say feeling bold. "Shoot me in your underwear."

He pauses and considers this. He fiddles with his camera and for a moment I think I've gone too far. He looks uncomfortable for the first time since he stormed in and took charge.

"I've never done that. But I'd like to, yes," he says.

He sets his camera on the floor, very gently, like it's really precious. Then he stands up, sighs loudly, and quickly removes his shoes, pants and shirt.

"All right," he says, not looking at me but picking up the camera, strong again.

His underwear is cotton. He is so tall, it hangs half-way down his thigh and I think it would probably fit me like pants. He is a full foot taller than me and I imagine my head would rest on his stomach. His cock is semi-hard. It's all I can do not to stroke myself, but he's already shooting and telling me positions to lie in, resting on one arm, pushing my neck out. It's hard work and my body begins to tremble and ache and I forget about the sex and really want to get this right for him. I'm leaning back and he wants me to push myself up on my elbow while keeping my chin down and also making my legs into a V.

"Why don't you come position me?" I say.

"No," he says.

I eventually get the pose and he seems happy. I want to have sex with him in the worst way. But I also actually care what he thinks and what he's feeling, so I don't just lunge at him like I do with most of my fuck buddies. I truly believe he may have the rare combination of traits to move beyond anonymity: sexy, sane, single and that something extra, the unnamable chemistry thing. He has paused with the camera and I realize I like this man. I find him incredibly intriguing and I think briefly of my short-lived therapist, a pudgy German woman, who identified what she termed my deep-seated intimacy issues and tried to get me to explain what attracted me to a man. I wish I could call her now.

"Can I kiss you?" I ask, still lying on the floor.

He steps backwards and looks me dead in the eye.

"No, but if you want to do something. I would like to watch." he says.

He moves back another step, leaning against the little counter in the kitchen. I spread my legs and I start to manipulate myself and he is watching, expressionless. I'm stroking myself slowly and feeling an utter tenderness toward him. I really want to touch him. I start to get up.

"I don't like to be touched," he says, reading my mind. "I only watch."

I take this in, and figure there will be a way to get around this soon, and I might as well finish my show for him. So I lavish attention on my cock and moan and groan and stretch my toes out, then spurt a big arc as his eyes grow a little wider. I think of how I can seduce him with my cheesecake and how nice it will be to cuddle with him through the long cold nights and how all of my dark, ugly behaviors will evaporate as he learns to be touched, and takes hot baths with me, and lets me feed him cheesecake in bed.

This is not what happens. He thanks me, packs up quickly, gives me a card with his number, and exits without even a handshake.

december 16

EVER SINCE THE shoot, I have been obsessed with Swan Man. Despite his cold exit, I still believe he has immense possibility as a lover. Nothing he's done really indicates this, but I feel it in my gut. There's something slightly off about him, an aura of screwy mystery. I too am a mystery. And there's something else, a sense that he saw into me and captured me. Maybe it was the camera, or the memory of that Irish boy in the tent. Or maybe I'm at the edge of a magical life-shift aligning me with Swan, as the planet Sexoid implodes in a far-off galaxy, scraping its lunar scalpel into my bitter, blistered raisin heart. Whatever it is, I'm convinced he's special.

    I invite him to dinner, which makes him quasi-real. We communicate through text, though, so he slips back a bit toward faceless hook-up. His texts are short, mature, solid:

german meatballs with sauerkraut.

That is his response to my question about dinner. I am older, more jaded, but in our text-play he is worldly, sophisticated and deep. 'German meatballs with sauerkraut,' sends me into a frenzy. I am at work, finding multiple recipes at cooks.com and also a foreign noodle dish called spaetzle. I make a shopping list and decide to buy cutlery. I only own two forks and one butcher knife. Blind Suzy keys-in on my bright mood.

"That's love in your voice." she says, tapping her blind-lady cane and getting ready to launch into a song.

It's at this moment, printing another recipe for meatballs at my sad little work station, that I have a crisis. A text from 'Super Blue Eyes.' He's a headless Grindr trick with a flawless, lily-white body, a smoothly luscious chest and a lower lip that promises lusty kisses. His profile picture cuts off at the edge of the lower lip, but I'm convinced that he's utterly stunning. I've been pursuing him for two months.

tonight at 8, ur place is all his text says.

There are so many, long, rancid encounters with fat, lost, doped and angry men. So much hunting and disaster. So many endless baths looking at the horrible edge of my black hole. And now, two beautiful options in one night. I have to act fast. Super Blue Eyes will disappear quickly, tripping back into the vast man-meat vat of Grindr. I send a text to Swan Man.

on for dinner.

The 'send text' thin line on my iPhone screen glows then disappears as my letters sweep magically to Swan. I consider setting up a date with Super Blue Eyes then canceling if Swan replies. Or a three way, a wild nude tangle. The text comes from Swan.

yes of course.

Super Blue Eyes will have to wait. I feel a rush of hope. This is what it means to be in control of my life. To turn down a headless body for a man who will come to my house for homemade German meatballs. I'm certain I will break Swan's

Diary of a Sex Addict

bizarre no touch barrier and teach him true love. This dizzy inner giddiness means something.

THE GREASE IS flicking its nasty finger at me and the stove flame looks dangerous. I don't know where to dump the grease so I pour the cream mixture over the meatballs and the whole thing sputters and screams, hissing and spattering onto the kitchenette wall. The cream also globs on the backsplash, white and gooey and I think of cum. The noodles are limp and pale, floating in a gray pot of water.

I've set two plates on my counter and laid my new cutlery. I consider adding napkins when the buzzer rings. He enters with very little fanfare and immediately I feel ridiculous, juvenile though I believe I am 10 years older than him. I realize I don't know his name but can't recall if he told me or not, so I am afraid to ask. He looks at my neatly-set countertop and very slowly raises one dark eyebrow.

I imagine he will launch into something unexpected, something happy, How enthused he is to see me, how thrilled to have German meatballs, his deep desire to stay the night and lie close to me and nibble pieces of me—earlobe, lip, nostril. But that chocolate eyebrow lowers, more a nervous tick. He stands still, waiting.

The evening is going to be like this.

He sits and dully eats my greasy, globby meatballs and paste-like pasta. He glances away often and sighs a lot. I babble at first, asking questions about his photography and Switzerland and, and, and. Then I stop. I eat silently and think of my mother, quiet and nervous, and my father, distant and cold. Those silent sad dinners. Those years.

Suddenly I reach for his hand and I yank it to my face and hold it on my warm cheek. I do it quickly, without thinking and he at first is still. His large skinny hand is on my white face.

Long snaky fingers, bitten-down nails, resting like the end of a slap on my cheek. Then he stands and topples his stool and goes to the door.

"What is the matter with you?" he says with emphasis and control.

I have nothing to say because to me he looks beautiful. I want to feel him shake in my arms. With my tricks from Grindr, Manhunt, the phone line, I am powerful and in control. At this moment, I am incredibly weak. He can see this, which I think gives him courage. He knows I want him. I'm completely thrilled with this foreign, sick feeling I have. He is the one. This is what they write about in romance novels.

"I don't like touching," he stammers, his hand on the door knob.

For a moment, I perk up and thrust my shoulders back. I've caught him.

"How do you have sex then?" I say.

"I don't," he says. "I photograph people. I'm celibate."

It's not the answer I expected. My years of brutal seduction are a waste on him, this priest-like fiend. He smiles at me and looks utterly calm and confident and I want, not to hold him or feel him tremble, but to be held, to feel him or even more, in a more immediate way, I want to be like him, to be aloof and untouchable. I despise this feeling, and suddenly, myself.

He raises his hand in a bizarre, boyish-like wriggling of his fingers, waving goodbye. The grease-stained German meatball recipe I printed from cooks.com which was sitting near the stove, flies in the air and flutters to the floor in the breeze that blows in as he opens, then shuts the door quickly.

I sit on the floor. On the wall, the world of my advent calendar looks bruised, shivering, like creatures from the island of misfit toys. I don't have the strength to hang today's eye-lid sized pair of ice skates.

december 17

I WILL NOT get out of bed.

Earlier, I opened the medicine cabinet, emptied the bottle of Vicodin onto the closed toilet lid and counted—twenty-two tablets. I don't know if it's enough to overdose but I imagine it could be, and I don't have the courage to find out. I will not eat.

I wake several times, vaguely recalling precise details of really violent dreams. An ax, weeds, the edge of a well bubbling with black blood, a chainsaw, slapping then punching then biting a man's ear off, and finally dislodging a pretty little boy's eye-ball and touching the smooth inner heart of his painfully tearing eye socket.

The dreams are a good sign. Anger is much easier to handle than depression.

december 18

I AM CRAWLING out of my skin. It's as if gallons of raw, illegally-potent black market espresso is main-lining through my veins. The strangest thing, the most insane part of it is that I do not want to have sex. This enrages me. I can only blame celibate Swan, who has not contacted me since abandoning my German meatballs.

I'm on the Second Avenue bus, headed to work after taking a sick day. I cannot stop thinking of Swan Man and his heartless rejection of both me and my dinner. I bought new cutlery for fuck's sake. He refused to even touch me.

An elderly woman gets onto the over-crowded bus and stares longingly at me. I have a seat in the very front, a spot marked for the elderly or disabled. Fuck her. She stands, teetering, looking as if she is going to moan in pain. I smile.

Swan has ruined me. I will soon begin to torture small animals and laugh heartlessly at sickly old women.

I honestly don't get it. I have been rejected by tricks thousands of times, and have also shooed away so many fat, old, withered, thin, young, foreign, or just oddly unappetizing men. This one rejection, this Swan, has me reeling and I can't quite figure out why. The thing to do, what I have always done, is to get back on the porn-fueled pony—ride nasty cock, swing into a beefy binge, obliterate all traces of this one bad 'Swan' apple.

The fact is that I have not been able to even get a whiff of a hard-on since Swan left my place. This fuels my original dream that he is special, that we are meant to be together. Luckily I slept through the day and night and avoided the extreme sadness of my black hole, and that alluring bottle of Vicodin. I know I cannot survive long without sex. At least this is what I have always told myself. It has always saved me.

I am determined to reach Swan and sort this out. Or maybe take the Vicodin, or shoot myself. The concept of suicide has never frightened me, but it also doesn't sound that enthralling. Plus, I have no idea if I actually have enough pills or where I would get a gun. I could mistakenly shoot my ear off and look like Van Gogh, though I have no idea what he actually looked like. I think Jack Lemmon played him in the film.

The thing is, I often linger at the lip of my black hole, close to sinking, to giving up. Then I begin my triple-threat sex hunt and regain my sanity. Swan Man has somehow set all of this off balance and he's not really even that hot. The only thing I can do is find him and (I suppose) force-fuck him. Have him over and drug his coffee then plow his bung hole. I wonder how long it has actually been since he's had sex and if he would ejaculate huge amounts, passed out in my arms? I have to admit, his celibacy intrigues and frightens me. I don't like to look at things I feel I could never personally do.

I refuse to acknowledge the old bitch still standing near me desperately reaching for something to cling to as the bus sways and bumps over pot-holes. She looks like she's going to collapse any second. I blame Swan for making me mean.

I shut my eyes to block out the woman and decide that I will find Swan and get inside him and make him break down, or I will destroy him. Or he will fall in love with me. Or I will turn celibate like him and we will live happily ever after. I realize I don't necessarily know the difference between any of these options. I just want him. And I vaguely understand that any of these choices may lead to my demise somehow. I've never been so obsessed over so little. As I said, he's really not that hot. I haven't even see the size of his cock.

A fat black woman stands up and gives the flailing old broad her seat. This cocoa fatty scowls at me and I scowl back. Fuck them both. I've had a hard life. It's not easy being a sex addict. I want to turn to the fat black woman and ask her how many men she has fucked this week. I bet none. I'm beginning to get off on being an asshole. I send a text to Swan. My entire body is itchy with espresso-like anxiety.

I need to see you.

I send another:

I have to speak to you.

As the bus trudges down the avenue, I text giddily, feeling near to Swan for the first time since he left me butt naked and sad.

It's really important.

Then:

Can I call you?

I consider this tactic a good one, a mild bombardment:

I can't get through the day unless I talk to you.

The old lady sitting near me is humming to herself. I text:

It will only take a second.

I don't know if granny is singing a church hymn or the theme to an old TV sitcom. I text:

You left something at my house.

I'm thrilled at my deception. The old broad is getting louder. It's the theme to the '70's comedy *Three's Company*. I lean

Diary of a Sex Addict 59

very close to her and whisper,

"Shut the fuck up."

And text:

It looks valuable. What you left.

The bus has reached my stop so I hop up and don't have to deal with the old woman's' very slow but overly dramatic reaction to my cussing at her, or her looking to the fat black woman for help. Fatty is a little intimidating and has probably socked a man or two. I send a last text to Swan as I exit the bus and head to work. I'm sure this text will snag him. The freak.

I'm celibate now too. It's my new thing.

I realize my anger has snapped the lock on a creaking little trap-door into a bizarre self-commitment to something utterly insane. It may not totally be about Swan, but I will work hard to make it all about him.

Take that Bishop Butt-fucker.

THE LADIES ARE having an anger management group today, lead by a withered looking lesbian who smells of cat piss. I put my hand to my face as Cat Piss Lady passes.

She looks at me with what I register as rage. Ironic. She is a guest from a radical group called Angry Voices of Women. The whole thing seems a little mixed up. Blind Suzy sings happily as she wanders toward the group room, and I wonder if she is as happy as she sounds, or is just faking it. I have typed in her case notes, so I know about her abuse, her being locked in a closet, her being blinded with acid by some asshole lover. They shut themselves in for the group room for a solid hour and I am alone with Google. I'm searching.

Celibacy is defined as the lifestyle of someone who is, and is striving to remain, unmarried all his/her life. It is also used to describe a state of life where one chooses to abstain from all sexual activities (also known as "continence"). Often, it is incorrectly used to refer to a mixed, an involuntary, or even temporary abstinence from sexual relations – celibacy is by definition a freely chosen state of being unmarried and practicing sexual abstinence.

Holy shit. Wikipedia is so wrong with its long-ass, misleading entry about celibacy. I wonder if Swan wrote it. This really freaks me out. I type my next Google entry quickly.

Sexual addiction refers to a phenomenon in which individuals report being unable to manage their sexual behavior. It has also been called "sexual dependency", and "sexual compulsivity." The existence of the condition is not universally accepted by sexologists *and its etiology, nature, and validity have been debated.*

I print out both Wikipedia entries to compare. The sex addiction definition sounds flighty, ethereal and unreal. What the fuck is a sexologist? I'm both insulted and relieved that the sex addiction definition is so lame. The Celibacy thing bothers me.

Celibacy is by definition a freely chosen state.

I'm trying to wrap my head around this. I don't like the use of the word free with celibacy and the word condition with sex addiction. Wikipedia sucks. I consider what my Wikipedia entries would be for these words: *Sex addiction is freeing and fucking hot. Celibacy is for lost and lecherous old priests who have no free will.*

I can hear Blind Suzy singing through the closed door. Anger management must be going well.

I text Swan.

celibacy is by definition a freely chosen state. hot.

I'm pretty sure this will intrigue him. He has yet to respond to me today. I've sent 17, no, now 18 texts. He must be lonely being celibate. I can't imagine he has a lot of friends. A louder voice, the cat piss lesbo, is telling Suzy to be quiet which makes me angry. I, of course, am never invited to attend the women's groups. I fantasize that Suzy lifts her blind stick and violently beats the Cat Piss Lesbian group leader to death, singing and emphasizing the lyrics with each fatal whack. This makes me smile. I do not feel guilty about having vile thoughts.

I type a few combinations of the word celibacy and sex and land on Saint Agnes.

Diary of a Sex Addict

According to tradition, Saint Agnes was a member of the Roman *nobility born c. 291 and raised in a* Christian *family. She suffered martyrdom at the age of twelve*[2] *or thirteen during the reign of the* Roman Emperor Diocletian, *on January 21, 304.*

The Prefect *Sempronius wished Agnes to marry his son, and on Agnes' refusal he condemned her to death. As* Roman law *did not permit the* execution *of* virgins, *Sempronius had a naked Agnes dragged through the streets to a brothel.*

I find myself getting aroused which is really strange. Agnes is a female, a child and a saint. I should not be feeling like this. Again, I blame it on Swan.

As Agnes prayed, her hair grew and covered her body. It was also said that all of the men who attempted to rape her were immediately struck blind. When led out to die she was tied to a stake, *but the bundle of wood would not burn, whereupon the officer in charge of the troops drew his* sword *and* beheaded *her, or, in some other texts, stabbed her in the throat. It is also said that the blood of Agnes poured to the stadium floor where other Christians soaked up the blood with cloths. She is the* patron saint *of* chastity, gardeners, *girls, engaged couples,* rape *victims, and virgins.*

Wikipedia gets points with this one. I should tell Blind Suzy about Agnes. Maybe Swan wants to be a saint.

Normally I would have spent this 'alone' hour posting pictures of myself on Grindr and maybe even hanging up my "Gone to Lunch" sign and running out for a local quickie.

I shut my eyes and register a scent of shit. None of the women have stepped out to use the bathroom. I imagine that the lesbo group leader snuck in a horde of cats so they could shit all over the place. The smell of shit is growing stronger, more pungent. The group is silent. I exit Google and shut my eyes again, sniffing. It really smells terrible and for a half second I wonder if I soiled myself, like some desperate old diaper wearing man. Maybe I summoned the wrath of an ancient Shit God by questioning the good work of celibates, while heralding the evil doings of sex addicts.

The group room door flies open and the women quickly

file out. The lesbian leader looks frantic and our program's chief social worker emerges from her office yelling.

"Get out, everyone get out now!" she says.

I shut off my computer and am the last to exit.

BLIND SUZY IS in front of the nondescript door to the domestic violence center and her eyes, though milky from her eye disease, look incredibly sad. She's holding her seeing-eye stick like a loose, rubbery appendage that will dissolve at any moment. Normally, she's tapping the stick and singing.

"I got to go home," she says.

The center is flooded with sewage. The place is funded by the city and connected to a ratty housing project. There are always problems. Some pipe exploded and sewer gunk has started seeping in. One of the social workers who spritzes her plants a lot is explaining the situation. We will be shut down until after Christmas. We are asked to take our sick and holiday pay and return in the New Year. Apologies are plenty.

I pass Blind Suzy as I slowly drift away. She is cussing softly.

"What the fuck now," she mutters.

I often wonder if a blind person knows when they are truly alone, or if they sense when someone is passing. I wonder if Suzy is celibate. I wonder if she loved her abuser or has ever seen true love. This makes me think of my ex-boyfriend, my only boyfriend, Ben. We were together for nearly six months. I keep a box of journals I wrote during our relationship locked up in my closet. I try not to think of Ben. I have not thought of him for a good long time, thanks to my constant hunt for sex. We broke up over a year ago. I suppose, in some ways, I hope Swan may be his slightly off-kilter replacement.

I creep quietly past as Suzy throws her cane on the ground then stands alone, teetering. I realize how much the center means to Suzy, and how much it fills her time. We are both going to be a bit lost. Swan has still not replied to my texts which hold steady at 22. I will miss Blind Suzy.

The sky is lit, and lovely, with a coming snow storm. I unlock my bike out front, mount and slowly ride away.

I AM EXPERIENCING alternating fits of rage and despair. I'm stricken with the fact that I'm out of work and have no savings, no lover, not even a regular fuck buddy. I'm headed to Auntie Flora's for an unannounced visit. Not for the expected hug of a loved one during troubled times. Rather—my thoughts run to murder and money. Her death could solve a lot of my problems.

The snow is light as I speed up the west side of town toward the old bat's place. I imagine sneaking drops of poison into her tea. I could pick up ginger snaps and inject them with cyanide. Or I could just stab her repeatedly with one of the elegant 18th century brass swords hanging in her living room, gutting her like a flailing trout. The trouble is, I'd get caught. No inheritance in prison. Though possibly some hot rape-scene sex.

Evening has come. I hope she's home. I pass a hardware store and slow down, thinking of stopping in just to look at the poisons. I actually have no idea where you buy fatal liquids.

I speed ahead, fantasizing about the funeral, the reading of the will, never having to type another disgusting domestic violence note about blind women and nefarious men. Never working or worrying again. Living in her elegant apartment, renting gorgeous hustlers by the dozen, all with huge inflated growth hormone enhanced pectorals. These boys would never speak, just parade around forever erect and yearning. I'd keep Lottie on as a servant to clean up after orgies, and serve ginger snap cookies in memory of Auntie Flora.

I park in front of Auntie Flora's and zip past the door man. He nods, and my murder plan deflates further. An assassin would wear a disguise, or at least use the back door.

I let myself in with my key. Auntie Flora is nibbling on a light supper in the living room, sitting erect, her eyes bright and alert as if she were expecting me. She waves me in, not at all surprised by my unannounced visit.

She's eating sardines on white crackers and drinking wine out of a long narrow golden chalice. Her assistant, Lottie, is nowhere to be seen. I sit in my regular spot on the fainting couch across from her, and wonder if smothering someone is easy or difficult—on, let's say, a scale from one to ten, ten being nearly impossible.

"I know what you're thinking," Flora says, downing her wine and tossing an oily bit of fish into her mouth.

She does not offer me any food, not even a glass of water. She leans forward, like an anxious little girl ready to reveal a naughty secret.

"You're thinking of that disastrous dinner with your mother, and that awful little brother of yours, the perverted little nut," she says. "I knew you'd come tonight."

I have no brother. I recall a few big family dinners during Auntie Flora's summer visits. I look around for medication bottles but see none.

"I am constructing my memoirs," she announces, revealing a bottle of wine which was hidden somewhere out of site. I believe Lottie once told me Auntie Flora was not allowed to drink. She fills her chalice.

"I want to get the juiciest pieces perfect. You know the dinner I speak of? But you weren't there. It was your younger brother."

I am silent. I don't know if she's drunk, or increasingly senile. I've come to regard Auntie Flora as a woman truly in decline, increasingly hopped up on meds. I suppose this should cheer me up. If she's slipping, we could start to make funeral plans.

Flora takes a very long, deep inhale then pushes out her breath as if she were a wolf blowing down a straw hut. She is a large woman, a fact accentuated today by the tremendous amount of fabric in her silk floral dressing gown. I notice she is barefoot.

Diary of a Sex Addict

I sit back, suddenly despondent and wanting to leave. The fact that I have no job, have endless time on my hands, have a seemingly impossible goal of celibacy all hits me hard. This fat woman is quite perky, eating sardines in a chair. She's not going anywhere soon, senile or not. She'll probably live to be a hundred and two. She'll likely outlive me. Maybe I'll will her my porn collection.

"I want you to hear this. I want to check my facts, it's crucial that I get this one right because I think it may have lead to your parent's problems," she says.

As far as I know, my parents had no major problems. They were in love to the end, or at least mildly content with one another. Waiting for her to begin, I realize I actually never heard my folks say they loved one another. I never saw them kissing or hugging. They were always separate, she doing the laundry, he outside doing yard work. I just presumed things were going well.

Flora pulls out a big yellow notepad, which must have been hidden with the wine. She is shuffling through pages scratched with pecked sentences.

"It was dark. We had dinner very late that day. But why?" she says this, a bit too anxiously. "It was extremely hot. Does that sound right? But you weren't there. That awful brother of yours was."

I realize that I am the awful little brother. I am the bad boy she wants to forget. Why she created a sibling for me I have no idea. Again, I decide to go with it. Truth is, I really have nowhere else to go right now.

"Yes, but my brother told me the story later," I say.

Her eyes fly open and she throws her head back with laughter.

"Oh I knew this was right. I knew it," she says, eyes back at her notebook.

"Your father made ribs on the BBQ. Your mother made corn on the cob and a peach pie. These details make the story richer I think," she says. "We were at that amazing antique table in your parent's dining room. It was dusk. Your mother had been drinking."

I gradually begin to remember the night she is talking about. I was ten. I recall a picture hanging above my mother's head. It was needlepoint, which she made herself. It was not very good, meant to depict a flower garden. But she'd run out of her colored threads so the whole thing bled into a mess of yellow. I had spent most of the dinner that long ago night staring at that needlepoint hanging above my mother's head, because I did not want to look at her face. I think she was crying, or at least trying very hard not to cry. I now know exactly what Flora is talking about, but she has it all wrong. My mother did not drink. Flora, however, back then during those hot summer visits, drank whiskey. Often.

"Your mother was wild and drunk. She stood up and knocked a picture off the wall," Auntie Flora says, a little too loudly. "She was that out of control. I think it was a picture of flowers. And she screamed at me. Get out of my house you harlot. That is what she said. I was devastated."

I remember that I was fondling myself under the table, wearing nothing but a pair of shorts my mother had made from an old, red-checked table cloth fabric. Flora was sitting next to me. She was rambling, which I think was normal when she drank. My parents ignored her. But something happened that night that upset my mother very much. At one point, thinking no one noticed, I had put my hand into my pants, and squeezed very hard on my tiny penis.

"Your mother accused me of fucking the minister. Some stinky old man, a widower. Your father did not utter a word, which was the cruelest cut because he was my brother and should have protected me. And *your* horrible brother, I think he took his pants off and ran out into the yard. He was disgusting."

It's all crystallizing at a rapid pace for me, like a watery rush of images, a slide show being force-fed into my mind. I remember that Flora was not eating that night. She was pretty drunk when dinner started. My mother initiated a gentle conversation, asking Flora where she'd been all day. Flora took this as an insult, a deep probing into her personal life. It hadn't been the minister though. It had been a local mechanic. Flora had lifted a glass of whiskey to her mouth over and over, and I had noticed black grease on one of her palms. She'd glanced at me once, noticing my hand in my table cloth material shorts, then cackled and downed her drink. She'd called my mother all sorts of nasty names, accusing her of prying into her affairs, of wanting her money, of judging her. She'd called my mother a frigid country-fried bitch. Flora was colorful when it came to phrasing things.

Flora is jotting something down in her notebook, and at this moment I really could strangle her. My mother had stood up, but not drunkenly, not knocking the needlepoint off of the wall, but tentatively, her shoulders hunched in fear, trapped. She'd stood at her chair as Flora speared out nasty insult after insult about frigidity and coldness and a woman's duties. My father had been stunned and tongue tied, though I think he was uttering something lame like "enough, enough."

I had squeezed my penis harder and harder until it seared in pain, unable to take my eyes off of the look of utter anguish on my mother's face.

I am now totally filled with rage, and as I stand up my body shudders with something like an emotional orgasm. I have never felt so angry and so sad at once. There is the sound of the front door opening. Lottie has returned. She is carrying a white bag from the local pharmacy. She looks at me as if I were a burglar. She notices the wine bottle. Flora looks stunned, child-like, lost.

"This is not a good day to visit," Lottie says sternly. "You should not be here."

I do not need to be told twice. I rush away, before I actually start to beat dear old Auntie Flora with my stiff and clenched fists.

IT'S TEN DEGREES and I'm weaving through traffic on my hapless little Huffy Five Speed like a suicidal snowflake seeking heat. I am aimlessly biking the city, like a blind man, trying to not think of Flora or my parents or Swan or my job or this series of increasingly irritating memories of my ex-boyfriend Ben that keep surfacing.

I stop at Barnes & Noble to look at sexy fitness magazines but am drawn to the religion section. I find an artist's rendering of St. Agnes in a big hardbound book called *Lives of the Saints*. She looks a lot older than 13, which is what Wikipedia listed as her age. But she is gorgeous with really long hair, and full lips. In the picture she wears a velvet outfit that accentuates her tiny girl waist. I look for something in her face that would explain her obsession with celibacy and God. Her eyes are cast to heaven, and to me she looks a little turned on. A very small nun wearing a blue gown and an old-school habit enters my aisle, smiling. She has the face of a gentle bull. Her features are large, exaggerated, her skin is heavily lined. For some reason I envision her hidden virgin nun pussy. This totally freaks me out so I bolt out of the store.

On the sidewalk, people hurry past in the increasingly heavy snow. Nothing has accumulated but the flakes are big and aggressive in the slapping wind. I've sent 26 texts to Swan. I love texting, and other than phone sex, really hate talking on the phone. I hesitate, then I dial Swan's number. He answers.

"Hello," he says.

His voice is slow, soft and steady. I can't begin to imagine where he is. I'm scared.

"Did you get my texts?" I blurt out.

There is a long pause. I can hear the wind in my ears and the shuffle of people's feet brushing past me.

"It's you," he says. "I don't like texts."

There is another pause. I don't know what this means. Did he read all of my texts and does he think I have something valuable at my house? Does he know it's me? I'm trembling. The bull-faced nun exits Barnes & Noble and stands near me. This is not going well.

"I can meet you and show you your pictures at the end of the week if that is good for you," he says very slowly.

"Absolutely," I say.

He names an Asian restaurant in the East Village and we agree on lunch.

"Good luck with the celibacy," he says, hanging up.

I stand on the sidewalk. The nun smiles and I imagine she's cruising me. I want to tell her I'm celibate and gay. I'm shivering. She lingers.

The mystery he presents to me, this Swan, has snagged me by the balls. He must think I'm fairly neurotic, having sent all those needy texts. He must believe I am trying celibacy and that I have something of his. Despite my fear, I am dizzy with the thought of our date. I realize that since ending things last year ago with my ex-boyfriend Ben, I have not had any actual dates, or conversations, or connections with other human beings only naughty, empty, nameless, angry sex appointments. This is obviously some sort of new beginning for me. This creature that is Swan is going to change me. I am hopeful. My eyes are wet and I realize I'm crying a little. The nun looks at me with compassion. I hate pity. I want to fuck her gaping bull-mouth brutally, to make the feelings go away.

AS I BIKE up a very long, steep hill through the snow, I busy my mind to distract it from the pain in my pedaling legs. I think again, a bit obsessively, of the word celibacy. I see the word in its four distinct syllables floating in the sky ahead of me, like it's the word of the day on a *Sesame Street* episode. The first two syllables are big and chunky to me, like Helvetica Cement. I decide these first two syllables, Cel-i, could be used as heavy stones to crush a body into the earth.

I pedal harder maneuvering my bike to flatter ground. The last two syllables of celibacy, ba-cy, are lighter and bouncier.

This is where I will land and heal, in Swan's embrace. We will end our celibacy commitments together, fucking like bunnies. St. Agnes will smile down on us.

I realize I am attracted to the idea of no sex, at least until my lunch date with Swan in four days. This can be a period of clarity and peace for me. Something utterly new. I can pray to St. Agnes for help. I formulate a fantasy meeting with Swan.

The East Village Asian restaurant will be empty, the lighting soft and dusky. A huge gold statue of Buddha will hover over us. Swan will confess that he is madly attracted to me and terribly lonely. I will take his hand and speak gently.

"I understand your fear, but you need to be touched. I am going to take care of you," I say. "I loved a man named Ben once and let him go. I won't do that again."

The fantasy collapses. A cab zips in front of my bike and I let rip a tirade of cussing. I am angry because I never allow myself to think of Ben, or how things actually dissolved between us. It is all vague and muddy, packed away in my memory box. I have never taken responsibility for how it ended. I just act like he never existed. I try to summon the Swan love lunch again, but it's ruined. I want to believe he will open my heart to love. Celibacy will clear my romance chakra, or something like that.

I'm not really convinced of any of this shit. My penis stiffens in my pants.

A truck skids in front of me and I pump my feet harder, a daredevil racing up the avenue in the increasing darkness of evening, unprotected, cars and angry trucks speeding all around me secretly hoping to send me flying on my gym-toned ass. The wind is gusty and ice cold as I climb another insanely steep hill that lines the East River, heading home. I can't remember the last time I spent a night void of sex or at least without the pursuit of sex. It has filled the darkest part of my mind for a long time.

At the top of the hill, I run a yellow light and barely miss the greasy grill of a barreling ten-wheeler truck. Pedaling faster, I decide I will buck-up and face the celibacy challenge. It may be the endorphins triggered with the biking, but who cares? I feel the rush of the engine's heat on my back as I climb higher and air pushes in and out of my lungs. This frigid air, this reckless driving is good for me. It will exhaust me and send me into a deep sleep. I will completely avoid my nightly black hole and that phantom bottle of Vicodin.

I LOCK MY bike and stand in front of my apartment building eyes shut, wind scalding my cheeks. My mind settles, my commitment flags. Can I actually do a night without sex, let alone four nights? I think again of my ex, Ben, and those journals filled with details of our frail relationship. They are buried in my closet. Maybe if I read the journals I will feel better, let go of Ben, move toward a new relationship with Swan. What would St. Agnes do? Sadness creeps in. I don't even know Swan's name.

I don't want to move, don't want to climb the narrow four flights to the darkness, don't want to go up there where nothing waits. Two chatty girls pass me arm in arm carrying shiny red holiday packages and I hate them. To me, they are stupid and fooling themselves to think that they are complete in their lives. There are wet snowflakes blowing onto my face. The drops die on my cheek and I know if I am celibate I will be alone for four days. Being alone terrifies me. Nobody is here with me now and nobody will be. Damn Swan, damn Ben, damn St. Agnes, damn Auntie Flora.

It begins to snow harder as the night sky fills with thousands of nasty little white eyelashes batting seductively at me. I trudge upstairs.

MY APARTMENT IS pitch black as I enter and stand alone as if in a cave. Trembling and cold, I wait for the hiding bats in my mind to swoop. It's very, very quiet. I move tentatively through my studio, thinking momentarily of Blind Suzy at work, inching toward the end of a dark room. I reach the edge, and I flick on the loud oscillating fan. My apartment is filled with noise and I can breathe. With the artificial wind, I undress, dropping my clothes, sweaty and damp from my bike ride. Standing nude I am slapped with the realization that nudity is the first step towards sex. I can feel every inch of my body, my skin tingles, my ass opens with a breath. The brush of my own hand on my leg is obscene and arousing. I press my arms straight out to my sides, holding them away. I'm ill, I realize, sexually ill and this makes me giggle in the dark. Nobody feels this way. Nobody is afraid to touch themselves alone in a black apartment where secret mind-bats wait to swoop. Nobody. Except maybe Swan. Or that mannish little blue nun at Barnes & Noble.

I flip the light switch and things brighten, the insanity drifts away, the bats rest. I put on a robe, sit on the floor and think of food. I consider sending a dinner invite text to my friend Michael, but it's dicey. Dare I ask him out to eat when he's trying to shed pounds? I could send him into a spiral at the mere mention of anything calorie related. Better skip it.

There is nothing else to do, no sex hunt to begin, nothing. I will have to eat at some point. The concept is overwhelming so I lie down on my back and shut my eyes for a nap. The last dish I cooked was German meatballs. That was not a success.

MY FACE IS pressed into hard wood and my lips are curling up cruelly and I can feel a bone aching and throbbing in my chin. It seems I am in some sort of 18th century stockade and my head is secured in a vice. They will burn me soon as a witch.

It's dark and hot and I've been asleep on the floor. I struggle up on one elbow then instinctively grab my iPhone and log into Grindr. As the postage-stamp sized images appear I groggily recall my celibacy but I don't put the phone away. I stare at my Grindr men. I just want to see who's online, who may have joined, who is in shape, who has a big cock or bubble butt or wears Speedos or spandex and, of course, if Swan is anywhere nearby. Is he here, is he alive?

I sit up in the dark, lit with my Grindr phone glow, and scan the men. No Swan. At the very bottom of the screen is a thin bar that says 'Load More Men.' The guys that appear on screen automatically are those closest in proximity. Starting with one foot (he's in the room) to 100 feet (he's in the building) to 500 feet (he's in the block) to 800 feet (he's down the street) to 1000 feet (he's in the neighborhood) to two miles (he's far away) to 500 miles (he's on a business trip). Each time you hit the 'Load More Men' bar, more pictures get added, but they are increasingly further away. I normally don't bother with this feature at all, but since I am not actually going to hook-up with someone, it seems like a good distraction.

Load More Men.

The bar swirls and slowly little squares pop up and the number of faces increase. I will need to begin to scroll down to see more fellas.

I've never really looked at the names that appear at the top of the tiny pictures. I'm usually busy texting and luring the biggest, closest cock into my mouth. The screen settles and I take my time with their names.

Billy.

Sounds cute. So normal.

Masc Lawyer.

Straight forward. Maybe rich?

John.

Dull.

Pie Face.

Say what?

I hit Load More Men again, wondering how many guys I can actually keep loading, imagining them slowly piling up one on top of another, creating a little mountain of lithe bodies. I sit up fully and catch the names and pictures as they appear.

M4M. Jet Setting Brit. Friendly Guy. Comfort Zone. Parker. Flrt. Alex. RR. Bucky Martini.

That one halts me. On occasion, someone is witty or cute and seems to honestly not want sex. I realize, being celibate now, I'm joining this Grindr fringe subcategory.

Load More Men.

Zoolander. Just looking. Zone Z. Ctown. JonJon. Asian Flu. Nuts. Bob. Pete. Mr. Magoo. Life Sucking App. Nice Man. Funny N Furry. Bombay Fox. Gotham Guy. TM. Ad Me Now. Quebec Man.

My eyes are fluttering. Swan is nowhere to be seen. I'm tired.

Load More Guys.

California. 79 Street. Xmen. TM. Turtle Pie. Boy Scout. Sam. CK. JR. BT. Antoine. Fireworks. Bubble Butts Now. The Visitor. Daddy. Popsicle.

I lower my head to the hard floor, barely keeping the phone up in front of my face, eyes loading, mouth loading, body loading, jaw loading. The mountain of men is growing immense before me. I see them piled, like boys, like men, my eyes shuttering open and shut like a camera lens as the phone drops heavily and I can see the limbs and the witch burning and the men piled higher but naked now, nearly skeletons and they are muscle and flesh and skin peeling off bones and there are athletes and boys and Nazis and nuns and Jews and smoke from an oven and the burning of lovers and priests and Asians and babies and Santa Claus and Lottie.

Load More Men.

R2. Azec. Phoenix Tears. Auntie Flora. Beatrice. Me.

Load More Men.

Alien. Nuke Me. Menace. Flow. P. Jim. Daddy. Stop. Mommy. Stop. Abu. Stop This. Mandarin. Stop This Please. Load More Men.

There is nobody here.

Diary of a Sex Addict

december 19

I REMEMBER THESE white chattering skeleton teeth that bounced around on a table one Halloween and made me sad. I'm still on the floor, in my dark apartment, but those teeth are bouncing toward me, toothy killers coming to eat me alive. The thought wakes me and I sit up, disoriented, wondering if I'm in the center of a lovely sex binge at 3 A.M. The dim, grayish light through my blinds tells me it's morning and I'm pretty impressed with myself for having slept on a hard floor, and not waking again, all night after the witch dream. I'm struck with an equally impressive wave of utter emptiness, similar to my black hole night-time haunts. There is no need to shoot naked pictures or post sex ads on Grindr or even go to work. I have three days of celibacy until my lunch date with Swan.

Sitting up, I grab a pen and jot:

Ten things I will do before I die
Kill an animal
Love someone back
Go to India
Fuck a mannish nun

The pen hangs in midair, waiting, like a knife poised to plunge into the heart of a terrified and angry lover. I'm feeling oddly violent this morning. Why did I write 'kill an animal?' I am not a vile person, but I believe in following through on the first spontaneous thought when I write. My mind is vacant. I can honestly only think of four things to do before I die. And they are all fairly awful, other than India. This day is going to be endless. I dress quickly, hang a jolly little elf's bootie on the advent calendar, and go out to see the snow.

IN TIMES SQUARE, the most crowded and distracting spot I can think of to hide, the parallel Avenues of Seventh and Broadway are black and slick. The snow stopped, but left a layer of ice. The sun is strong, bouncing off of the polished pavement and the wind is bitter and strong. The tourists are ridiculously happy. I huddle in a corner near the entrance to Toys 'R Us. There is something uncanny and otherworldly about these people. They smile and wander and do not notice me. They are chatting, and the children are missing gloves and eating pieces of Hershey's chocolate. I hear snatches of conversations: lunch plans, museum schedules, stores to visit. I've slipped into a wintry little bubble, absolutely separate now. I imagined, incorrectly, that being in a crowded spot would take me closer to humanity and away from my obsessive desire for something to happen, anything to happen other than sex.

I see a woman's very round white face. She has paused with her husband and two sons to look into the toy store window and she is telling her husband that the Ferris wheel in the lobby 'just can't be real, it just can't be real.'

"It's a mirage," I say firmly.

She snaps her head toward me, this strange man in the corner, a gray hidden pervert that could grab her teenage son and gobble the edges of his wrestler stud ass. Her big round blond face tilts to the side, like one of the oversized dolls in the store window, and half of her mouth creeps up into an ugly smile. She tilts her head the other way and keeps tilting her head back and forth, as if trying to gain momentum so she can come up with something to say. I notice her taller teenaged son, who is also very blond and muscular and is wearing a high school jacket open at the nape of the neck to reveal the hairless edge of his pubescent chest. The woman is searching for something to say when her husband pulls her away. The family disappears.

A hearty wind makes a high-pitched squeal and the crowd yelps with delight. I check my iPhone and see that it's eighteen degrees. I start to walk quickly East toward my apartment, the frigid wind snapping around me. I realize the blond woman upset me. I hate her. I would really like a big cock in my mouth right this minute.

I try to recall why I am so determined to be celibate. I stop and feel the wind at my back nearly knocking me down. I am celibate because of Swan, though obviously he would never know if I fucked men and bull-faced nuns endlessly until our lunch date. I think this shift is a challenge to myself. Swan is simply the force that tore into a secret piece of me that I am now crawling toward. I know, also, that it has something to do with Ben and the unopened box of journals. And maybe that bitchy Auntie Flora.

I realize for a split second that I am actually really, really tired of having sex. I stand still with this thought for what feels like a very long time. The light goes red green yellow red green yellow many times.

❖

I'VE REACHED THE Lord & Taylor department store. Swarms of tourists are filing behind red ropes looking at the holiday window depictions of tiny figures ice skating. The window's scene is set in the 1800s. I can see, in the corner of the Lord & Taylor window, a ten-inch man in a plaid suit skating on a glassy ice pond. There is a fluffy toy dog near him, the pup's head bouncing up and down. My fondest childhood memory is of ice skating at a local pond. This was before I began to think about sex. We'd go, my father and I, right after he got home from work. It was in a park, I think, and I was very small. There was a trash can filled with wood and paper lit on fire, to keep people warm. There were big billowy green trees near the pond. Mostly men were skating, in dark brown skates. I never stepped onto the ice. My father was young then and very lithe and a good athlete. I had tiny wool mittens with a bear's face on the front. The bear's eyes were like tiny, sad bits of coal.

A little girl has smacked her head too hard on the Lord & Taylor window, as if she was trying to crack the glass and crawl in to kiss the little skaters. She is wailing now but the other tourists in line are not moved by her cries, they look at the child and her mother with disdain and push the line forward. The girl's eyes are open very wide and she looks a bit insane to me, though lovely with ringlets of blonde hair and a tiny red velvet coat. I think of St. Agnes and I imagine this impatient line of holiday shoppers pouncing on the child, slicing her head off and tossing it to me like a football. A saintly souvenir.

I dart away quickly, crossing the street, thinking of my father and his pretty brown skates and the powdery snow around the edges of the pond where I would sit and watch. A cabbie blares his horn and rams his fat bald head out of the window screaming something ugly, but with his horn beeping I barely hear it. It sounds like he is saying 'flowers flow on.' It may be 'fucking moron.'

❖

AS I TRUDGE across town to the safety of my apartment, I notice a swarthy Latin man studying me at East 38th Street. My celibacy commitment feels safe, since I rarely pick up men on the street. I used to, before all my websites and phone hook-ups and iPhone and Grindr connections. Ten years ago street pickups were a gay norm in neighborhoods like the West Village and Chelsea. Cruise, smile, find a spot and fuck. That's how we sniffed each other out. Dogs smelling asses. Not anymore. It's all online.

The swarthy Latin is still eyeing me. He is definitely way past twenty, but bug-eyed sunglasses, an elegant cashmere coat with a giant sable collar and a hat reveal so little skin that he could be anywhere from thirty to fifty. His wool pants are tight around the crotch and I am pretty sure the hand in his pocket is fondling a nice set of nuts. I don't need this stimulation. The wind is pressing at me, and my celibacy commitment wavers a touch as my cock stiffens.

Luckily, across the street is a church. A big white-washed stone building with a lean metal cross glistening on the roof. The man in the sable collar is moving swiftly toward me, smiling like he may speak. Mildly panicked, I cut through oncoming traffic, cross to the church, and bound up a small set of stairs toward sanctuary.

Inside, light dissolves into artificial night. The church is empty, cavernous and cool. Wide rows of blonde wooden pews flow gently to a broad and clean alabaster altar. There is a skylight above the altar, a skinny scepter of sun shining like Jesus' damning finger or his sharp, erect penis.

I take a deep breath and let myself sink into the silence. I spent the formative years of my life in church. My mother sent me to the local Fayetteville, Arkansas Catholic school named St. Henry (patron saint of the handicapped and those rejected by the religious order). That cheap ass place was more like a wooden barn with a few candles and pews. Wind shot through the walls during mass often blotting out the priest's religious babblings. In that dim, cave-like place, I often fantasized about the grade school boy's near me, at least the ones that didn't wash and stank of morning chores, the ones with tiny muscles growing in their dirty little arms.

As I move slowly toward the alabaster altar, the door to the church opens. Mr. sable coat strolls in, hand still in pocket, fondling. This is a moment teetering between titillation and ten commandment terror. Sable coat man is eyeing me and I swear he is licking his lips like a horny serpent. This is what they call evil blasphemy. Fucking in a pew. Blowing a man next to the plaster Virgin Mary. Cumming in the holy water dish where elegant old widows will dip jeweled hands on Sunday.

He's standing very still, staring me down, and as arousal flutters, I realize I must escape. I recall hiding in St. Henry Church, long ago after mass, to avoid being corralled out to recess. I hid in the confessional booth.

Sable coat is taking a step, and I move toward a bank of stained glass windows and a row of confessionals. The wooden booths are connected in sets of two, one for the sinner, one for the priest listening through a shared screen.

I don't look back, turning the gold knob and stepping into the black solitude. I can hear and smell my own breath in this dark, hot little hovel. I imagine sable coat man scratching at the door, panting and growling like a rabid devil dog. I have a sudden desire to press my tongue onto the screen and see what it tastes like. This dank, linked confessional tomb reminds me of the buddy booths they have at porn shops around the city. Those booths stink of sweat and cum and have scratchy porno playing on 'pay as you stroke' tiny screens. The buddy booths are side by side, divided by a panel. With the touch of a button you can cause the dividing panel to spread open like an ass, a glass plate revealing the man on the other side. You can masturbate for one another as long as you keep feeding the porn machine dollars. When the money runs out the divider snaps shut and you are left in the dark, which is depressing.

These are not the things I should be thinking about in a church confessional. I should leave, but I feel trapped, stuck in this four-walled coffin, afraid to face the sable coated cock demon on the other side of the door. He's probably lounging lewdly in a pew, stroking himself. I am overwhelmed with a dark rush of scented memories. I feel sick, as visions erupt with force, and I remember not just St. Henry and athletic altar boys and buddy booths, but a church last year, and a wedding with Ben.

At that wedding there had been a few torturous moments when I'd considered going to confession, laying out my infidelity, asking for help. I'd started to sweat, while one of Ben's nieces glided up the aisle. I began to tremble and cough. I was hot and overwhelmed with a desire to blurt out everything. Ben had squeezed my hand for a moment. I'd shut my eyes, bit my lip, and it passed. Sort of.

There is a voice muttering through the screen. I wonder if it could be the sable coat man, coaxing me like Lucifer to sweep over to his side and get naked.

It is a priest.

"Forgive me father for I have sinned," I say, the line recalled from years past.

I can't quite hear him, nor can I see anything. He wants to know something, he wants something from me. I used to lie as a boy, making up things I imagined regular farm boys would say. Innocent things. But I can't lie right now, I can't make anything up. I can barely speak.

"I'm..." my mouth is moving and there is bile rising to my throat and I realize I may vomit. "I'm so scared."

I bolt out of the confessional, and make my way swiftly to the exit. There is no sign of sable coat man. The priest, if he really existed, is not chasing me.

I am alone again on 38th street and I am going home. I make a note to avoid churches in the future. Nothing, it seems, is safe anymore.

❖

THE AFTERNOON'S LURID cathedral horror has left me in an odd state. I'm sitting at home in the dark. My iPhone is off as I doze on the sofa. In the shadow near the hissing radiator pole I see a rat. It scoots out, sits on the floor, then scurries on little legs under my large glass-door paneled bookcase. The brutal winter wind is pressing at my window and I hear again the high-pitched squeal of frigid air blowing. I rub my eyes and sit up. The rat is under my Crate & Barrel, very expensive, yet-to-be-paid-for bookcase. A few months ago I threw a used condom under there and left it as a badge of perversion. I wonder if the rat will eat it.

I stand up and know, in my softer mind, that there is no rat. I am half-dreaming. It's not possible. Yet, I cannot go look under the bookcase afraid of both the imaginary vermin and the dead condom which must be hard and yellow like a brittle leaf. I've been sleeping most of the afternoon.

I try to make out, in the mix of sounds coming at me, the distinction between the harsh outside wind, my hissing radiator, a slight buzzing in my head and a gnawing sound, which of course would be the imaginary rat. The fact is that, in my apartment, I often hear strange noises, but always late at night. Never during the day. At night, I am usually waiting for a sex date, feeling safe and cocooned in a fantasy of what he will look like. Will he be hot? Will something dangerous happen? This stirring in my mind, in the dark night, makes the noises I hear unimportant. The door slam of a neighbor several floors below, a crash that I imagine is a cat knocking over a trash can, the typical siren, the beat of music from a party or a car passing. It's all background to my racing mind, my sex mind that will soon send me to stand butt naked at the door, peeping through the door hole, waiting for my appointment to arrive. But that's deep into the night, not mid-afternoon. And I've never imagined the sound of a rat chewing.

Diary of a Sex Addict

I have not even made it through one full day of this celibacy thing and I am imagining rats and small girls being beheaded in front of Lord & Taylor.

I am suddenly very tired so I lie back down on the sofa, realizing if I just crawl on my hands and knees and look under the bookcase my anxiety will pass. But I can't. I rest on the sofa and glimpse a blue haired rat climbing out of my black hole as I drift off to sleep.

I WAKE AND through the wall the neighbor couple is making noise. They are having sex, or arguing. There are loud voices, singularly, then overlapping, then it goes bleak and quiet. The voice of the woman, a perky blonde girl who I have glimpsed looking so small and firm like a Russian gymnast in the hall, her voice rises to a crescendo. A perfect slow rise to a crescendo. I begin to wake and seethe. This vanilla-sweet couple is having sex, thrashing around through the wall, while I am celibate. How dare they?

It's silent again and I imagine they are slowly twining, naked leg over leg, a foot touching an ankle, a bit of blonde hair stuck in her mouth that he pushes away. A hand cupping below the midsection, soothing and tickling.

This quiet, and the thoughts of the couple, make me extremely edgy. I sit still and listen for the couple intently, but don't hear them anymore. I don't even hear my phantom night sounds, no strange cars honking or cans toppling. It is utterly still. The last insult: with my eyes squeezed shut and straining with all of my might, I don't even hear that imaginary little rat. There is nothing under the fucking bookcase.

I have got to get out of the house, and I am desperate enough to follow a suggestion my reclusive friend Michael made once, after I related a fairly raucous and I thought amusing tale of a wild three-way. He'd looked at me with the stern, horrified concern of a rehab counselor and told me about a daily Sexually Compulsive Anonymous meeting he knew of. He had sat through it once by mistake (thinking it was Overeaters Anonymous). At least it will get me away from the rat, and it's cheaper than a movie. I'll try anything once.

IN THE ELEVATOR up to the Sexually Compulsive Anonymous meeting I am shamelessly cruised by three comically out of shape black men who talk about me as if I weren't there.

"Well ain't she looking fine in them tight pants, mmm hmmm, all right now."

I sigh and roll my eyes for effect, then realize they can't see my eyes since I am wearing a pair of oversized tortoise shell sunglasses. The meeting is held at a drug rehab aftercare joint in Chelsea, and the loud black men get off ahead of me on the fourth floor, undoubtedly heading to their own life-saving counseling. The room designated for sex fiends is at the end of a drab dirty hall which is lined with ancient, tattered and greasy posters with slogans like Silence=Death and Fight for the Cure. The whole thing is too Keith Harring, I think, trying to summon a cynical stance before I enter.

It doesn't work. I'm trembling as I turn the knob and for a moment I think this is it, I am stepping into a new landscape of my life. I will change radically. My palm burns on the knob, my knees shake. There is an electrical charge scurrying up my spine like a starving rat racing toward his sex recovery cheese.

I stand humbly at the entrance. Many of the men in the stuffy little room are attractive. It makes sense. Attractive men have the opportunity to have way too much sex. Ugly men must go to Masturbator's Anonymous meetings.

I step gingerly into this room full of men who can't stop fucking, about twenty of them crammed together, close, knees touching, in folding chairs. I think of them all nude, tangled,

Diary of a Sex Addict

sweaty, a post-meeting orgy. I sit in the rear.

There is one very ugly man. He is in the back, against the wall, alone. His chubby leg is in a soiled cast and is propped up on a chair. His arms are folded and he looks like he would bite me if I turned to speak to him. I scan the room. In addition to quite a few humpy boys, there is a really obese black man with a pretty face sitting near the front. He looks oddly happy. Near him is a truck-driver faced tranny wearing a cheap red wig, a lot of makeup, and a synthetic pant suit probably from Kmart.

The rows of chairs face the front, where a striking brunette sits smiling. I recognize him from a poster for a local phone sex ad. In the ad he is topless and smirking and the text near his head encourages you to 'call in and get off.'

Today, he looks peaceful. The ugly man with the cast coughs loudly several times. His cough is deep, phlegmy and awful, like someone in a Tuberculosis ward. The men ahead of me, decked in skinny jeans and form-fitting sweaters, shift uncomfortably in their folding chairs as the old nut in back keeps coughing.

I am nervous and want to stand up and in my best Joan Crawford voice say "This ain't my first time at the rodeo boys." I want them to know I have made a concerted effort to change. This is not even my idea, coming here. It's fat Michael's. I think of all the self help topic books I have read (or at least scanned at Barnes and Noble one long, rainy Saturday) about sex, sexual abuse, sex addiction, sexual fantasy, sexual dysmorphia, sexual recovery, sexual intensity, sexual dysfunction, sexual origins, sex and intimacy, sex with a caring partner, sex in the church, sex through the ages, sex as a tonic, sex with yourself, sex as theatre, sex and fame, sexual transcendence.

My brain is twisting into disgusting phallic shapes.

The phone sex poster model in front is finally starting to speak. He looks gorgeous and positively vacant. His eyes are open very wide, but they don't register on anything in the room. He looks straight ahead and seems to be medicated. There is a soft, boyish quality to his voice. The ugly cast man yells from the back.

"Speak up."

The boy clears his throat, and begins with the same empty sing-song tone, but with the volume turned up slightly. He is gushing about gratitude and all that the meetings have done to help him and his life and his modeling career and his new relationship. I wonder if he's done any modeling other than the phone sex poster. Maybe a Vodka ad or a porn film. I wonder how large his cock is. I wonder how much sex he's had and with how many men. Remarkably he starts to tell me.

I am trying to listen, but zoning in and out as this fragile, dazed beauty talks earnestly in a deadpan voice about his life. He says he wants to share the last days of his rock-bottom. I think how I'd love to share his rock-hard bottom with every man in the room (minus gimpy in back, the tranny and the fat black dude), and realize at this point I am not likely to get anything substantial from this meeting.

I am just too deeply perverted.

Then he begins to tell his "worst night" story, that life-changing event that brought him to "the rooms and peace". The story involves a drug dealer who has sex with strangers in front of his fucked-up lover as a form of mental torture. Beauty was involved with the drug dealer in a particularly screwy three-way.

I am, of course, aroused, but as he speaks I follow a desire to step more deeply into the story with my own more visually intense interpretation. I am very creative that way. I try to listen to him.

"I knew that night, naked, having unsafe sex again it was all over," he says.

Several people sigh and shake their heads with understanding and the truck driver tranny moans strangely, then spits in a hankie. This is really stupid. These people are absolute fucking losers.

"I knew I could be stuck having sad, lonely sex like that until my luck ran out and somebody hurt me really bad, and I had a moment of clarity and thought there has just got to be a better choice, right?"

The tranny shakes her wigged head vigorously in agreement. The speaker is really irritating me now with his Lifetime Television Oprah Winfrey style crap, so with each sentence I slip further away, concocting an X-rated version. The truck driver tranny has her hands over her mouth, as if she is going to cry, as if she can relate so deeply to the handsome man in front. And I think: you are butt ugly and I want to yank your wig off, you are not at all like the speaking beauty. The tranny is rocking in her seat and I am guilty for a moment, sure my energy is going to pollute the entire room. Tranny is going to sense my wretched thoughts and turn and hiss at me.

I have lost all hope of any internal discovery here.

The speaker says they were in Chicago, a city I've never visited. He's using words like hope and courage and self love and self loathing so I slide down a deep little hill into my soft and trashy comfort place.

I decide to see it cold and bleak. All shades of gray. They are in the drug dealer's house. A sleek metal high rise. A sparsely decorated living room. Big windows looking out onto a high-rise filled city jammed with coke snorting addicts and crooked horny cops. The drug dealer is nude and has his legs spread wide open on a white leather—no a black leather—sofa. I've decided he's Italian, very machismo, olive skinned and brutally handsome. I'm actually just visualizing a porn star I saw on an internet site called Dirty Tony but who cares. My drug dealer is a big Italian brute with a gigantic cock and he's all coked up and going to teach his dirty little bitch of a boyfriend a lesson by fucking our phone sex poster beauty in front of him for hours. The hot and nasty boyfriend will be forced to watch, but won't be allowed to touch himself. They will tie him up then pump him with Viagra and he will weep and gnash his teeth.

Up front, the morbid beauty is actually relating a similar story, though not with the titillating details. I feel ever so psychic. His version, however, keeps overflowing with saccharine platitudes and he seems to purposely avoid lush little words like fuck or cock or suck or lick or ass or rim or cum.

"He used me, to teach his lover a lesson. I was his plaything and I have never felt so empty," Beauty says.

I'm still mildly turned on but need to press on my cock through my pants to keep my dirty mind alert. I don't care who sees me do this, though all eyes are riveted towards the front. I have to keep my eyes shut now because it's getting more challenging to stay in my fantasy. If I look at the whale-sized black man or the trucker tranny I'll slide way off course. Also, if I listen too closely to the speaker I will lose my internal smut rush.

"When I finally got out of there, I called my Mom in Tennessee," Beauty says softly. "I was so, so, so fucked up and there was a blizzard in Chicago that night."

I can't stand hearing him go into detail about reuniting with his dear old Meemaw in a swirling blur of snow. I hum to myself softly to block out his voice and swap back to my version.

The dirty boyfriend is crawling nude across the floor on all fours, moaning and barking like a dog. He's crying and asking for forgiveness. The brute Italian, whose cock has grown to a foot long, is smashing it up the ass of Beauty and screaming at his crawling boyfriend to repent, repent, repent! The boyfriend knocks his head repeatedly on the carpet until a cut erupts and blood dribbles into the plush and outside, a silver jet screams past, rattling the walls. The drug dealer has grown stubby red horns atop his head and his cock is becoming impossibly colossal. Floating in the window is the leering face of Jesus with a crack pipe between his lips.

I realize my years in Catholic School and my recent visit to that church are interfering with all this. It's getting muddy as the errant boyfriend fades, and the big-dicked Italian peters away and I am left with the stupid Beauty up front, who is crying quite brilliantly.

He has finished his story, which I sort of missed being lost in my fantasy, and the fat black guy has gone up front to offer him a tissue and everyone is clapping and these men, the hunks around me, actually seem to be moved deeply. A few of them stand up and hug one another. The black fatty is making announcements about a sexual retreat, which sounds ironic. The only one not affected is the ugly cripple in the back. And of course me. I am untouched. But my icy response is having an odd impact on my frazzled brain. My sluttish mind has gone horribly limp and I sense the arrival of my black hole. I have the same sinking sensation I get after a long binge, that bleak feeling that I cure with a Papa John's pizza or more sex or just sleep. For a brief second, I realize there may be someone else very near me who feels the same way and I think—isn't that why you came here fuck head?

The door swings open and a skeleton breezes in, carrying four Walgreen shopping bags, moving quickly toward a seat up front near the trucker tranny who is waving to her. This late arrival is basketball team tall and cancer-thin. Her hair hangs in long dyed-red shards around a face filled with bones so pointy they may poke through the skin at any moment. I am both numb and choked up, not because of the fat black man rattling on or the shuffling of the skeleton's shopping bags or the ugly cast man coughing in the back. I realize I have seen the skeleton woman. Her name is Beatrice and she's dying of lung cancer and she was abused and she came to a support group at the DV center where I work. She showed up once, then never came back. At my desk, as she left that day, she smiled and told me that I had beautiful, sad blue eyes.

I get up quickly, hoping Beatrice doesn't see me as I flee. No one in the room seems to notice that I've come or that I've left. Other than the cripple in back. He's glaring at me and I think of that weird fetish subgroup of people who like to fuck the stumps of amputees. I am truly In-Fucking-Sane.

I move swiftly down the hall, then break into a trot, vowing to never take advice from Michael again and hoping that Beatrice did not see me. I want to see the misshapen black men in the elevator again and have them taunt me and treat me like a sexy object. The elevator ride, however, is slow, quiet and lonely.

❖

IT'S A COLD, clear evening. I cabbed to the meeting, but am walking home. I am in no hurry to get back to the my apartment, that barren land of drab loneliness. Celibacy, it turns out, is a bitch to maintain.

I'm walking west, passing rows of brownstones with front windows lit warmly in holiday cheer. I'm moving very slowly, recalling an article I read about slowing down all your movements to calm yourself. The street is empty so I take each step as if I'm pressing through a wall of sand. I consider heading to Auntie Flora's but am still a bit wrecked from my last visit. I don't like all the memories she stirs up about my folks.

It seems to be working, this ridiculously slow pace, because in a brief flat moment in my mind, I realize there was a period of semi-celibacy in my past, immediately following my parents' death.

I never though of it that way, as I made no choice or effort to stop having sex. I just slipped into an odd neutral zone for a period of months after the funeral. I pause, my foot in the air above the sidewalk, shoe hovering as if I were a circus performer on a high wire waiting for the line to steady so I can step down safely. My foot lands and I take a deep breath. I'm feeling sort of spiritual then a thought crashes in that fucking ruins it.

I spent fifty thousand dollars after my parents died. In a short period of time, I spend a shit load of money. But I didn't have much sex at all.

My shoe lands on the sidewalk and I think if I press hard on the concrete I may just keep sinking down into the earth, past this city's sewers and subways to a black, wormy mud pit where my skeletal parents are sitting and chatting about the despair of their son's life.

The money came from the sale of their farm house, minus some outstanding debts. I'd never considered keeping the family home. Standing still now, I realize I never thought of us much as a family at all. They seemed happy, but I darted far away early on and imagined they thought of me very little. It didn't really bother me.

I have reached the front of an empty high school and decide to sit on a bench against a brick wall. I am trying to recall exactly how I spent all the money I inherited in such a short amount of time. I also wonder if I become rich after Auntie Flora's death, if that will quiet my urge for sex. If I spend nonstop, will it erase my sexual mania? I feel very analytical today. I rarely spend time thinking of anything other than sex, food or sleep. I'm quite a Neanderthal at heart.

Across the street an oak tree sways and I think again about how I spent all that money: there was the new furniture for my studio apartment and the Bergdorf Goodman credit card and clothing spree, the pile of home appliances, a bizarre contribution to the city's Society Library, the constant spa visits and of course the lavish trip to Egypt.

And the hustlers.

The last several thousand was spent on rent boys. I conveniently blocked that little tidbit from my memory book. The wind has stopped completely and this seems like a cruel trick. To silence the world around me on an empty street on an empty bench. Fuck you Mother Nature.

I recall the flat, though comfortable place I inhabited during the time it took to rush through my dead parent's cash. I was not exactly numb. My physical body was quite alert. I was filled with a spending energy and used up a lot of time planning what to do each week and month. I was not working, and I don't recall feeling much emotional pain, rather I was very focused and productive. There were lists and charts and plotted-out days. A breakfast cappuccino at Nespresso the elegant Madison Avenue coffee bar, a new Jil Sander mohair sweater at Bergdorf Goodman, a facial at Juvenex Spa.

The oak across the street from me is swaying its branches in my direction, which makes this cold, dull moment feel less brittle and lonely. Was it just a terrible waste, that spree spending? It did lead me to a scarred-up and empty place where I was open enough to land in Ben's lap after all those hustlers and the intensity of Egypt.

And the Egypt trip was worth every cent.

The hard oak across from me suddenly looks puny as I think of visiting the island of Abu Simbel in Egypt. The trip overall, in memory, is a mad swirl of extreme heat, massive monuments, and a dark aggressive people whose eyes I was told repeatedly not to look into. I was on a five star, extravagant tour that went from Cairo, down the Nile to the Valley of the Kings. What I most recall, though, is Abu Simbel.

A small boat took us to that island in Nubia on the Western bank of Lake Nasser at dawn dropping our small group to wander down a broad path tangled with purple flowers, toward a mountain of stone. Reaching the mountain, and turning the corner, I was so struck by what I saw I had to sit and literally catch my breath. I could not move. It was a Pharaoh and his wife, seated side by side, carved into the towering mountain. I'd seen scads of huge amazing things on that trip but this was a new level of awe-struck wonder. It seemed an impossible creation, and in the sun, unable to move, just staring at it, I knew the stone couple were eternally united, and then, my parents, often so expressionless, yet severely united, were also now never apart in death. They had been a unified force my entire life, and I had been something outside of that, mostly by choice, and in their death, the structure that gave my life its center dissolved. They however, remained in unison.

That is not exactly what I thought, sitting there in the one hundred and ten degree Egyptian sun, but it was something like that, just more jumbled. There was a whisper of that, some blur of my folks recently dead, some murmur that dropped a seedling that began my slow trend toward a deep desire for a solid and stony relationship, which was Ben.

I think once I got back to New York, my subsequent spiral

into rent boys was a feeble attempt to erase that desirous germ that was planted that day at Abu Simbel. I gorged on a certain type of boy, between eighteen and twenty, always Latin, always excessively endowed, always with overly big lips and inflated pectorals and big empty eyes. Perhaps that too was a reflection of that stupendous Abu Simbel monument, all stone and hardness, over-sized and Godlike.

The last boy I rented was Egyptian. I laugh aloud now, the mighty oak across the street is motionless. I hadn't connected it all back then, had just seen his profile and chosen him. I swear his name was Abu. Or am I making that up? It could have been Rocky, or some other fake tag like Brutus or Angel.

He was young, his cocoa skin was very soft and he wore blue contacts and kept his hair short. His work-out regime was enhanced with steroids and a trendy growth hormone so his pecs and arms were way too large, utterly cartoon-like, in contrast to his small waist. His very large cock was his own. I was obsessed with his inflated, unreal body; he was my rent boy crack.

Sex with him, the last of my saved money gone, marked the real beginning of my porn fascination, my constant hunt for uber-sex, my dull need for out of reach and ridiculously overdone men. The thing is, that desire can't really be quenched, unless you buy it or work with porn stars. The exhaustion of all that lead me eventually to Ben.

I have a terrible headache. I will never make it to a celibate lunch with Swan if I keep flashing into these ugly memories, these needy obsessions. I think again of the white box of Ben diaries at home in my closet, and as I stand to go, bidding farewell to that poor tiny American oak tree, I know they need to be dealt with.

december 20

I'M AWAKE, AND in a brief bright moment, as a thin thread of daylight comes through my blinds I feel utterly rested and very hopeful. I am just waking, and I can't recall how old I am. And I feel that there is someone dear to me standing close by. I feel happy and want to stay exactly as I am. But the radiator hisses, and there is a gentle recognition of what that is, that noise, the neighbors, the imaginary rat. This leads me further toward myself, this apartment, the animals in my head and Swan, the failed Sexual Compulsive Anonymous meeting, my angry visit with Auntie Flora, my black hole and my ex Ben. My life, in just a brief moment, has gone from simple to incredibly complex and a bit awful. Plus I have a hard on.

I sit up and realize it is day two of my celibacy escapade, and two more days until my lunch with Swan. I'm aroused but not stroking myself, not reaching for the phone or the internet to find a trick. I get up, stiff cock bobbing and walk proudly into the kitchenette. I put a red star on the advent calendar then stare at my toned body in my big Ikea mirror and think: I can do this. I can make a choice. I can stay celibate and even forgive nutty Aunt Flora. I can succeed. I am not a total loser. St. Agnes would be proud.

I try very hard to believe at least some of this.

I can hear, from down the hall, the sound of Christmas carols. It's muted, but I am pretty certain the song is "The Little Drummer Boy" rum-tum-tumming his way into my apartment. I immediately think of fucking him, this teen shepherd boy with an ugly drum around his neck on his way to visit the Christ Child. I think of throwing him down near his sheep on a grassy knoll in Jerusalem, fucking his dirty little Drummer Boy ass until he screams in his native tongue. I don't know if they are screams of pleasure or horror. I don't care. He thrashes in the grass, dark skin all awash in the night sky, sheep coming close to watch us, sniff at us, me nude and thrusting harder and harder and smelling the stink of an ancient civilization climaxing up his nasty asshole.

I shut my eyes and say a quick prayer to St. Agnes then drink several glasses of water. I keep my eyes closed and my familiar black hole appears in a giant flash as my cock softens and dies. I lean on the sink and I can see the edges of my black hole. It's volcano-huge now in my mind, bigger than it has ever been, and there is swirling smoke and a claw reaching out to me. I haven't thought of it this intensely for awhile. It is appearing to me more often, and during the day which is unnerving. During celibacy, I don't have my sexual escape to save me.

I finish my water as the black hole dissolves and I acknowledge that I really have to eat. That will help my mental state. I am frightened by the celibacy vow but also excited that I'm actually doing something that feels nearly impossible and incredibly tough. Years ago, I liked to challenge myself.

I stare into my small refrigerator, enjoying the warm glow of the inner fridge light spilling on me. There is nothing but a fat cucumber, large and deeply green. I reach in toward the cool, lit space, then pull back. I don't know when I bought that thing. I think of feeding it to the imaginary rat, or trying to stretch the old brittle condom lying under the book case over its circumference. I hate cucumbers, and likely bought it to shove up some fantasy drummer boy's ass. I reach toward the cool inner shelf and lift the green organ, but can't bring myself to sniff it. I need to go to the store to buy food.

GROCERY STORES ALWAYS feel safe. I am distracted by the narrow rows of colorful cereal and cracker boxes, huge piles of fruit, shelves of bottles and cans. I wander the aisles in awe at the numbers of items shoved one on top of another, mating. People are very internal, rushing, grabbing, shoving things into tiny baskets to get away. Couples seem distant, like they desire utterly different items but are forced to compromise on Wheat Thins over Cheez-Its. Everyone seems cold and determined and I warm to this. I move slowly, savoring the space, headed toward frozen foods.

I grab two Red Baron pizzas then wander happily over to dairy, looking for cinnamon buns in a can, the ones that plump in the oven. Rounding the corner, I am halted by a pile of pound cakes. Some clever sales clerk has created a circular tower of these wrapped treats rising up on a table at least three feet high. They are the cheap pound cakes, the Tabletop brand, tightly wrapped and featuring a smiling girl with pigtails. I can't move. This is the cake Ben bought for us every Saturday night back when we were a couple.

I can't turn away from that daunting pile of pound cakes or the sudden memory of Ben. He used to serve me this pound cake with hot cocoa, in bed. I found the whole thing wonderful—the taste of the soft cake with the hot chocolate, the thrill in his eyes as he served me like his pet cat, the satisfaction as he sat next to me and we devoured our sweets.

I am normally expert at refusing all memories of him. He had disintegrated in my mind. But something, obviously, remains. Thankfully I am blocking the way of a tight-buttoned bitch in an expensively tailored suit. She grumbles and barks as I turn and head to the check out, far away from those awful little pound cakes and that sugary, ugly little pigtailed girl.

I AM UNHINGED over those horrible pound cakes. They have shoved me right up Ben's ass.

I force the two frozen pizzas into my mini-freezer then sit in front of the closet for awhile. Stored in a big white box on a top shelf are the series of diaries I kept over that six month Ben period. I have never looked at them, and feel no good can come of reading them. I know, however, that I am going to look at those journals soon. Just not yet.

I head out to the gym because I cannot sit still and have lost my appetite. I desperately need to distract myself and get back on track. I can't let my celibacy commitment crack. Two more days until my lunch with Swan. I am proud of myself and irritable. I choose bland sweat pants and a loose T-shirt and hope the gym is empty.

I fantasize that while I'm gone the imaginary rat will sneak out from under the book case and chew up all of the journals. I will find him dead and bloated with those sad, tiresome memories.

I will bury him in an unmarked grave.

december 21

IT IS JUST after midnight and the snow has come back, batting those white slut lashes at my window. The white box, tightly wound with packing tape, sits in front of me and I am naked. My apartment is very warm, and the radiator has been hissing for quite a while.

I have given in to Ben and the diaries. Once awakened by the pound cakes the packed away memories were too alluring. I also have an incredible amount of free time on my hands and am still too pissed at Auntie Flora to go see her.

I stare at the white box. I'm not afraid. I will read these things and then burn them. It will be another ritual, similar to my celibacy journey or my late night baths. I will destroy that part of my life, and I'm sure this will trigger the universe to bring Swan and I together. I will invite Ben to our wedding. The black hole will permanently disappear. I will feed the Vicodin to the imaginary rat.

I haven't eaten all day. The pizzas are nestled in my freezer, and I know I will have to eat eventually, but I also know that Gandhi fasted for quite a long time (at least in the movie) and he turned out fine. I'm enjoying the gnawing empty feeling and mild light-headedness from lack of food. I lie back for a brief rest and run my palm over my stomach. My abs are flat and hard. I wish I could have worked out, but my earlier trip to the gym was a disaster.

Typically, when I am pressing weights with tiny curls of sweat on my legs, eyes, arms and chest, I feel this surge of power and sexual energy. I thought I could just breathe through that bit of nasty triggering, and push through a workout. I also thought the gym would be empty with Christmas approaching. It was not.

The men at my gym are almost exclusively gay. They wear the craziest, sexiest outfits: short-shorts, sheer spandex, bike shorts bulging, fashionably tight-fitting sweats, tank tops that scoop down way below their tits showing off naked firm chests. Nobody looks at anybody but everybody studies everyone. You can spy on someone while they are grunting and lifting a huge barbell. I usually study the men in the mirrors, licking them in my mind while their eyes are shut mid-grunt. Also, everybody has sex in the steam room. I suppose I should have had the fore-thought to know the gym is not a good place for a celibate man. This afternoon, I only lasted fifteen minutes.

I was curling a barbell, working my biceps, when this Mexican kid stood directly in front of me. I could smell his cologne, he was that close. It was a citrus and woody mix, maybe Tom Ford's 'Extreme.' He had very short black hair, big lips and the kind of body that has recently shifted from chunky to muscular, so everything looked particularly full and plump and bursting. He was wearing a tight-fitting spandex tank top, and miniscule white spandex shorts. He stood close to me all citrus and woody, stretching his arms over his head, eyes shut, his tank inching up to reveal a trail of tar-colored belly hair sneaking down into the mound of his big fat cucumber crotch. The cucumber made me horny, but also hungry for a salad since I hadn't eaten in such a long time. I fled, out of the gym, tromping through a flurry of falling snow, the cold clearing my head. Once I got home I stripped, sat on the floor, and finally felt ready to face these Ben journals, in front of me now.

The white box is not easy to open. I remember I bound them like I was burying Dracula, never to be brought to light, never to be released on an unsuspecting village. They were meant to stay in their white cardboard tombs until the end of time. The tape won't budge so I get a sharp knife. As I lift it to slice the tape, for a brief second, on the dark wall ahead of me, my black hole flickers in shadow and whispers and I wonder if the knife is sharp enough to slice my wrist. I stab the tape and take a deep breath, feeling a little dizzy. I am way too dramatic.

The lid slides off, and I hesitate, then shove my fist in recklessly like I'm fisting a drunk boy's anus, pulling out a secret locket shoved in their years ago. The first diary is in a Hello Kitty notebook. It's bound with three rubber bands.

I'm exhausted already.

I cut the rubber bands with the knife and they snap and fly under my bookcase with the rat and the old condom. I do not look at the far wall because I know my black hole is trembling the same way my hands are trembling as I open the journal.

There is a smiley face. I want to vomit. I have trouble remembering any time in my life when I was happy enough or stupid enough to draw a smiley face. I flip randomly through the pages.

There are no dates. The penmanship is erratic, child-like: blue then red then pinkish ink, colors shifting within paragraphs. A section is written in bright green marker and stick figures are drawn with what must have been a greasy orange crayola. There is a smear of chocolate and one page is filled with pictures of young men in swimwear torn from glossy magazines. There is a tiny matador wearing an elaborately brocaded cape, grinning.

I do not recall compiling this retarded pile of shit.

For a moment I am struck by a vision of myself wearing flannel pajamas. There is a notebook balanced on my knees. I know this memory, it has been with me, but muted. It was two years ago, when I met Ben. That was me. All cozy and eating pound cake and jotting orange crayola ideas in a notebook.

I can see through my blinds as a steady flow of snowflakes blow aggressively in the increasing storm. The flakes look dirty and gray, not at all like the soft clean snow dusting the pond where my father used to skate. There are too many of them, millions of tiny ice-fleas racing to splat on the sidewalk below. I want to yank open the window and throw these boxes at the mass of repulsive snowflakes. I look at the ugly snow, then at the colorful journal. I think again of the rat under the bookcase and my last sex binge with Speedoboy and Pig and of Ben and Swan.

What the fuck has happened to me?

I MET A guy named Ben. A funny little man unlike any other. At least he's not at all like Wilhelm who was mean. I was Wilhelm's bitch for a month but I got away from that nutty fuck. Ben is sweet. I am ready for love. A fortune teller told me last month that love would come, but I would try to destroy it. She wanted more money to explain how I could avoid destroying it so I told her to screw off. I hope she didn't curse me.

Ben and I met in a sex club in a two level bar way downtown. My friend Joe, who traffics with trannies and porn actors and poets, runs the place as an underground after-hours hang out. I wonder why I noticed little Ben? I think I was over the dark ones, the angry men like Wilhelm who dumped me because I wouldn't let him put his cock up my ass. What a pig he was. Ben had a gentle aura.

That night I thought—I want something lovely and nice. So in came Ben.

At this point the ink changes to pencil. I decided to change from ink to lead. It's coming back to me, my line of thinking back then. When my father died, he gave me a drafting pencil. It was thick and red and all scratched up with his teeth marks. He used it to hold it in his mouth when he was thinking, as he drew construction plans. He was a carpenter when he was young. I think I wrote segments of this journal with that stupid thing because I thought it made it special, with his teeth marks and lost saliva. For some reason, I also switch to present tense with the pencil-scrawled stuff. There are several wet spots on the page, brownish, which I believe are coffee. Undoubtedly, I was under-nourished and overly caffeinated, pushing me into this wired present tense state.

MEN STARE AT each other, some make out. Voyeurs linger in corners. I'm near a gorgeous blonde athlete. He has a very thick body and is surly looking. He's wobbling, quite drunk, and there's a smaller black man trying to pry his shirt up and off, but the blond hunk is not having it. He snaps his head toward me and grunts. At the same time I see this nondescript dark-haired fellow, lingering on the edge of the dance floor. This is Ben.

As I move toward the blond, I keep an eye on Ben. He has a tranquil look, like he's watching a pleasant film or listening to a symphony.

The blond smiles and I press my mouth toward his armpit, and suck in his scent. Ben is swaying to the music and sipping a brightly colored beach drink. He moves a few steps toward us. The big blond stumbles a little.

I pry myself away from him and shift over toward Ben. I begin to fondle myself and move against him. He does not flinch. The big blond watches, which turns me on, so I push open my pants and rub against Ben. He fondles then jacks me off pretty efficiently. I ask him to come to my place and he accepts matter of factly, as if I've just offered him a mint. We are silent in the cab.

At my studio, he excuses himself, goes into my bathroom and vomits, then comes back to my waiting bed and falls asleep very quickly. I watch him sleep, insanely intrigued because he is so ordinary, which to me is un-

usual. I have thus far known only nuts, drunks, derelicts, fetish lovers, brainless athletes, fools.

He is going to be my lover, I think. He is perfectly boring. He will never leave me.

THERE ARE A number of pages in the journal with red and green hearts, smiling faces and a little house drawn in blue. I wonder who this brain dead teen girl is who hijacked my journal. She is obviously naïve and thinks she is in love. She is experiencing a rush of new and exciting warmth, something like the feeling I had when a trick pissed on me for the first time last summer. She believes this feeling is going to last forever and that some new world has opened up to her. This girl who has known nothing but emptiness, sex tricks, chaos and loss thinks she has found love. She is in for a big fat ugly awakening.

BEN IS A foreign object, a creature that I've never encountered. He is so easily satisfied. I am so easily disappointed. We compliment one another. When he lies down at night he immediately falls asleep. He is snoring now and I write in a dim glow from my bedside lamp. It does not bother him.

I had him over to watch a scary movie and eat pizza, which is a perfect date. He said the pizza was bland and he fell asleep during the film. I watched him sleep for a bit, then woke him up to ask if he wanted to stay the night. He grunted and smiled and said sure thing. As he sleeps, I think of a unicorn, a glimmering and strange animal. That is Ben. I am discovering love. I think I will stay up all night.

I explicitly invite Ben over to have a bath. I love hot baths with candles and lavender. It's like an amazingly romantic offer. He strips and sits in the tub, then says it's too small and he's suffocating. He dresses, thanks me and leaves. I keep watching the empty hallway after he's turned the corner and gone down the four flights of stairs. I keep watching the empty fucking hallway.

❖

I AM FINALLY eating and my entire body shudders with each bite. I am gobbling my frozen pizza topped with perfectly circular pepperonis. My stomach is bloating with each greasy bite. As I munch, I study the guts of the white journal-filled box. A notebook with a grinning skeleton head intrigues me. I recall buying it when I was in a bleak mood. Maybe the giddy teen girl died and a brooding rock boy was born. I am trying to connect where I was emotionally then, when I wrote these journals, and how I got to this place now. I don't recall such a radical shift in my emotional life. I have, of course, always been moody.

I rip open the grinning skull notebook and am greeted with the handwriting of a mad man. Huge, frantic letters written in the smeary black ink of a half destroyed leaking pen. Shifts in tense and lots of big violent scratch marks, like I was digging the pen into the page trying to tear open the words. The first page of the skull notebook has three big words: I FUCKED UP!!!!!!!

This seems more like me.

I SO SO SO SO SO FUCKED UP. I AM FUCKED UP. I HATE BEING FUCKED UP. I'm going to wreck this shit. Ben is everything to me. I love him. Oh fuck fuck fuck fuck fuck.

What I did is killing me. Ahhhhhhh. I jacked off two boys in the rest room at Washington Square Park on my way to the gym. This, after three months of sex with nobody but Ben.

One looked like he was in college, the other was too young to tell and black. I can't be sure about age with black men. They confuse me. He could be 12 and well hung or he could be 22 and just very small, almost midget-like. But he was aggressive in joining what had already begun in the bathroom.

It was all so wrong I found it really intoxicating. I wanted to rip my

Diary of a Sex Addict 105

eyes out but I wanted to cum over and over. This particular bathroom is disgusting, a hang out for mentally ill homeless men. The mad men linger behind a wall where the shit stalls are, singing to themselves and speaking in tongues. The sex happens at the urinals. I hadn't been there for a long time. It was always a last resort, a dirty little pit stop after a depressing day.

The totally fucked up part is that as I left the bathroom, imagining a squad car waiting to arrest me for statutory rape of the black boy, Ben called and asked me to have dinner. I was thinking of him at the exact moment the phone rang as I stepped from the putrid bathroom into the light of day, so I see this as a horrifying sign.

"What are you doing?" he said.

"I'm at Macy's shopping for bath towels," I said.

He believed me. The stupid, beautiful fuck believed me.

We have sex that night and I am afraid I stink of the restroom. While he sleeps soundly, I hide in the bathroom and cry, then shower in scalding water and scrub my skin over and over, repeating, I will never ever cheat again. NEVER NEVER NEVER.

THERE ARE TWO pages ripped out in this skull notebook. The frayed edges remain and I have no idea why I destroyed them. I do know that I cheated again, over and over, dozens of anonymous little hook-ups. There is a red streak of something on the next page, and again, I do not know what it is. Ketchup? Pizza sauce? Blood?

I am drinking a big hot mug of coffee and thinking that it was smart to block all of this out of my mind. Who could handle memories like this? I know I fucked this up, but I am trying to remember Ben in it all. He had to know or sense something? He had to feel a shift. He was in the same relationship right? It takes two to tango.

If I had a series of personalities like Sybil in that really sad television movie starring Sally Field, I could blame it on the other people in me. Bob, Raymond, Benny, Bill. But I do not have that multiple personality disorder. I am only me.

Fuck.

I've been sitting still for what seems like a decade. I count the journals. There are twelve in the white box at my feet. The twelve days of Christmas, the twelve apostles, the twelve stations of the cross. This line of thought is freaking me out. I took the batteries out of my bedside clock and put it in the closet, because I want to forget about time for awhile, but it's unnerving. No daylight is coming into my warm little cave so I don't know if it's afternoon or evening but I can see the swirling dirty snowflakes.

I reach in and pluck a very nondescript notebook hoping it reveals something a little more pleasant. I don't know what order I wrote these in, so this could be before or after the Washington Square bathroom three-way.

TODAY I AM in one of my rare calm moods. It's raining.

The odd thing about thinking I'm in love with Ben is that I have never been in love so how do I know? Our sex is super vanilla. I've always fantasized about romance coming, the kind that gallops in and overwhelms you with tons of outlandish sex and sugar love. That is not what's happening.

I just think of Ben a lot, and thinking of him makes me smile. That's about it. Also, when I'm not with him I look forward to being with him. He comforts me like nothing in my life ever has.

The only problem is that I have been having anonymous sex. I stopped being freaked out about this for now at least, and have entered a deadly calm zone to keep myself sane. I just can't handle guilt for too long. I decided that since we never said we had to be exclusive it might be okay, but I imagine he is exclusive. And I want to be monogamous some day, but I wonder if I can be. I must be afraid of intimacy, because that is what I read in a self help book. Plus everyone talks about it on television as if it's this gorgeous thing to strive for. Fuck them. Lots of people have intimacy issues and often talk about them on daytime talk shows like Jerry Springer. I saw a show where a man cheated with his wife's fat sister. But I think the sister turned out to be a man.

The truth is, I am sure I have deep, untreatable intimacy issues, though I honestly could not explain what an intimacy issue looks like or point it out on the street. Regardless, I really do love Ben. I wish I could tell him the truth about myself but I know that would totally ruin everything. I feel like I'm spinning in a pretty little circle, a brain dead child on a merry go round, a skater on an icy blue pond spinning it its own mad orbit.

THERE IS A gap of many empty pages in this notebook. Big, white clean and lined pages. Very tranquil, like good snow. The snow outside my window still looks gray and dingy. After the blank pages, the writing begins again in blue ink, very neat. Almost like an essay being prepared to be turned in to a frigid schoolmarm, played by Emma Thompson in a film.

IN THE AISLE *at a huge Staples store downtown, lost, looking for a laptop cord and this kid is stroking himself. He looks Brazilian. He's very well dressed. We are in the basement level, late day, and nobody is around. We are in the very back section in a row of boxed-up software games with names like Zombie and Pit War and Street Fighter. His eyes are huge and brown, like a stunned doe, and he is licking his lips like a cheap internet porn actress and rubbing what looks like quite a package in his pants.*

I stopped in on my way to spend the weekend with Ben. He wants to cook for me. Cod fish. I hate fish but my heart is lit on fire with his cooking for me. I can't tell him I don't like cod fish. I am afraid of hurting him.

I stare at this Brazilian kid, his throbbing crotch, doe eyes and lips. I'm in the center of a little sex theatrical and for the first time in my life I really want to walk away. I put my hand on his crotch and my mouth on his lips. We make out for a long time as I rub him, wildly thrilled and petrified with the fact that we are in a store and could be arrested. Finally, he cums silently through his pants.

I tell Ben the train got stuck. He has been keeping the cod fish warm and he is delighted when I say it is really good.

I hate the taste of the fish and I hate myself.

We do not have sex that night. Just cuddle and sleep and I feel something irrevocably shifting.

At breakfast Ben talks endlessly about his job and his family and I'm not that bothered by it. I can't help but think of the Brazilian boy's crotch at Staples. We lie side by side that afternoon and he has this way of putting his legs over mine, like he's holding me down. I find this really comforting. I'm sure this is part of love. He brings me hot cocoa and pound cake in bed. I hope he's going to do that again. I think this is intimacy.

I try to stop thinking about the big-dicked Brazilian whore in the Staples store.

THERE ARE NOTEBOOKS surrounding me, spines broken, pages flapping like dying birds' wings in the wind of my fan. The white box is nearly empty. I am beginning to see what happened with Ben and me. I can glimpse pieces of the disintegration from a distance as if it were someone else. My cheating, his clueless trust, the ax falling. I turn on the television and find a show to give me insight. I leave the volume off.

There is a male host wearing a bowtie, an obese bleached blond woman crying, and a very thin young man standing near her. A skanky-looking skinny girl with acne is holding his hand. The fat blond keeps crying. The skinny man takes his hands out of his pockets and starts to wave them around speaking. The fat woman has buried her face in her hands.

I imagine he has cheated. He has left his fat lover at the trailer park while he fucked the skanky girl at Staples or in a restroom. Infidelity. It happens all the time. The fat woman is bowing her head low while the skinny man flails his arms. I can see that her hair roots are gray. She does not look old enough to have gray hair.

She suddenly stands, grabs her chair and charges the skanky girl, who has her hand on her hip. I turn off the television.

Maybe if I had told Ben about my cheating and my fears of intimacy he could have hit me a with a chair and I would have cracked open like an egg and my truth would have spilled out all over the floor and we would have sorted things out and stayed in love.

I sigh, then pick a pretty lime green notebook out of the saintly white box.

AT THE GYM. This hot guy standing near a weight rack wearing really tiny green nylon gym shorts and a spandex T-shirt asks me my name and I say it's Jack. I speak in this low, angry voice which seems to turn him on. I've seen him having sex in the shower room.

I see myself in the mirror reflection behind him and from this distance it is not me at all, it is Jack. Jack is not a very nice man. I smile at myself in the mirror triumphantly. My life is really coming together because I'm in love with Ben and I am in shape and I am desired by many men. I've got it all figured out now. I am one hot mother fucker.

I think I'm in my prime.

THE LAST TIME I saw Ben we sat across from one another at a diner. I did not know then it would be our last meeting. I told him I needed a break because I didn't now how to be honest with him and I had to find myself. He gave me a very, very blank look. It was like he was a plastic doll that could not move its hard stiff face. He said:

"Do you want me to wait for you?"

It was the saddest thing I ever heard and it terrified me. I told him I didn't know. He did not move his face, just got up and left.

That was the night I sat alone and knew I might never feel Ben's touch again, never eat his pound cakes, never have his legs link over mine, never taste his kiss. That was the night I first drew a lavender bath, counted my Vicodin, sat sobbing in the tub, and clearly glimpsed my black hole. That was the night I invited a stranger to come over and blow me. He was bald, steroid muscled, and dressed in a wrestling suit.

I'm staring at the white box. The snow is still falling. The journal entries are getting brief.

I HAD A dream that my ribs were connected to Ben's ribs and when I tore away my breathing stopped. Is this the love they sing about?

I'm reading "Looking For Mr. Goodbar." That trashy woman is nuts.

Ben gave me a slim gold ring. I wear it all the time and never take it off.

I AM VERY tired. The snow is heavy, creating a white wall outside my window.

The white box at my feet has become a gaping hole, obscene, like the little drummer boy's wide dirty ass. There's soot and shit and field grass around the tiny slut's full, ravaged ass and it seems more like a mouth. The box mouth is gaping so I press myself into it and feel the sunken, hungry sides already so full of abuse. I will fuck the corners, deep and hideous.

I am beginning to torture myself. I've been up all night with these journals.

I see a slender notebook with a purple dinosaur on the cover. There are no rubber bands, nothing holding it tight and secure. It is bright, and its pages have not yellowed like those of some of the journals. I realize it is the last one.

I snap it up, glad to jump to the end. I'm ready to light the whole box on fire. I lift the journal and a picture falls out from the center, a snap shot of Ben, New Year's Eve in Atlantic City, a casino spotted with palm trees and that awful mix of bright gray light that can only shine inside, in January. He's wearing a shimmering green hat with the words Happy New Year in gold. There is a cheap plastic horn balanced on his lips, though he doesn't seem to have the energy to blow it. His eyes make me shudder. They are utterly empty, absolutely sad, but also unaware and vacant. He could be a wax figure. This was before that final meeting at the diner. This was when I still thought it would all work out.

NEW YEAR'S EVE *and there is no midnight kiss. Only tacky Casino happiness, honking horns, fat women glaring at 'I Dream of Jeannie' slots and hairy pear-shaped men sipping free beer. This trip was my idea. Ben has just won two hundred dollars. I don't really care. We wait for the bus to take us back to Brooklyn, to his place. The night is over.*

At his place.

Ben is trying to snuggle and I can't stand it. I can only focus on the sounds through the wall. His neighbors are young and very fucking jolly. It's dawn and the sound of their lingering party, occasional laughter, this slow, sickeningly whimsical music coming softly through the wall. He has given up and rolls away from me, and I can feel him going even further, over the edge of the bed, then under the floor boards, then down deep into the earth, dead.

I am so incredibly tired and from the street I hear a boy's voice shout, cheering and then repeating a phrase and I want to pull that boy on top of me, to run out of this apartment into the icy cold and yank that boy shouting down onto the sidewalk.

I'm going to get up, quietly and sneak away. I'm going to go and pound on the neighbor's door and tell them to shut the fuck up. I'm going to go out onto the street and meet that boy with the shouting gleeful voice. I am not going to sleep.

Ben is snoring and the tiny, delicate sounds of other people are assault-

ing me and I can't stop thinking of the beginning when Ben's touch was like a tickling feather assaulting every nerve in my body. I am sinking so swiftly, it's like an elevator with cut cables, plummeting, soaring down. I'm getting up now, I try to tell myself. I'm leaving this place.

I keep lying very still and his breathing near me is calm. I am dead.

december 22

I AM MEETING Swan for our late afternoon lunch at an East Village sushi bar. His choice. It has been four days of celibacy. I slept a long time after my traumatic and enlightening journal reading binge. I am awake and refreshed, scraped clean and clearer than I have been in my entire fucking life. I've also had a lot of morning caffeine.

As I take my time, showering, choosing the right boot and a shirt and sweater combination that is both attractive and reserved, I understand why Swan has come into my life. He is a teacher, like Jesus.

Well, maybe not Jesus, but he is part of a bright new fate. The celibacy, the domestic violence shelter closing, the phantom nun I saw at Barnes & Noble, the fact that I have been without sex for four days for the first time in years, my revelations about how shitty I was with Ben, the fact that I could never tell Ben how I felt—it's all part of a new master plan. Once I move forward with Swan, I will find the strength and clarity to make amends with Ben and we will be good friends.

Despite a fleeting fear that I may be caught in a delusional heal-thyself infomercial, I believe this shift is real. That's why this morning I called Ben and left him a message. I'm ready to face all that. I hang a star shaped ornament on the advent calendar for December 22.

As I spritz with Tom Ford's Black Orchid cologne I have a delicious vision. I am a brilliant green fly caught in a shimmering silk web, realizing that my thread-like paws can lift and soar. It all adds up beautifully, my life right now. I can fly, like Santa's reindeer or Peter Pan. I swat away a thought of fucking that Never Neverland boy-man in his sheer green tights as he sits astride a Reindeer buck.

I will relate my fly vision to Swan at lunch. He will look at me calmly over bite-sized fish and say he understands me and feels a deep connection. I imagine he has been through an awful break up with someone, has found peace through celibacy, and is ready for new love. We are so similar, Swan and I.

I have a few hours before our lunch so I am going to see a zombie movie. Horror calms me.

IN THE FILM, the small Ohio farming town has blown up and the pretty husband and wife heroes are alone at a diner. They look movie star grubby, meaning they are stunningly attractive with a few soft pink bruises on their faces and their plaid shirts are artfully smudged with mud revealing the struggle they have gone through. Together they killed a dozen zombies in the past ten minutes. To clarify, the things they killed aren't real zombies. They are farmers who got infected with a government-made chemical that got into the town's water system. The chemical turned the nice farmers into homicidal maniacs. I suppose the pretty couple only drank bottled water, so they were spared zombie-ism.

The pretty man and wife, who argued a lot at the start of the movie, have been brought together by tragedy and zombies and are going to kiss now in the diner. They don't see the drooling Zombie Lady with the chainsaw approaching in the distance.

I am weeping, thinking of Ben. If only we had been thrown into a brilliant catastrophe, we may have begun to tell the truth to one another and seen the bigger picture of a life together and shared a long loving full-lipped kiss like the couple on the screen. Ben loved diners. A bloody, sawed off zombie finger soars across the screen and the violence startles me. This is wrong. I should be thinking of Swan, not weeping over Ben.

Two rows down from me in the nearly deserted movie theatre, a heavy-set balding businessman in a cheap suit lays his head on the shoulder of his tiny Asian girlfriend. He looks fragile doing this, his largeness on her tininess. This makes me weep again and I stifle a sob with my hand over my mouth.

The Zombie Lady has broken the hero couple's kiss by throwing herself through the glass window of the diner. She is chewing on the good-looking man's arm while the wife screams in horror then grabs a steak knife.

What I think is this: people just need someone to love. The rest is sort of stupid. I check my iPhone, which has been muted, to see if Ben returned my call. He did not. I will tell Swan about this movie and about my revelation about love. I think Swan will relate. I feel bright and hopeful and am pretty sure this is what I once heard Oprah call a "spiritual awakening" on an episode about obese women surviving mid-life crises.

On screen, the wife has repeatedly stabbed the steak knife into the Zombie Lady's flabby neck. Zombie Lady falls over foaming at the mouth, which is a good thing.

I sit alone in the empty theatre long after the credits finish and the screen goes black. An attendant comes in to clean, spots me and turns and goes. I wish he would have stayed and done his job, ushering me out into my life instead of leaving me alone. He should have waved or said hello or did something friendly.

Asshole.

THE EAST VILLAGE sushi restaurant is dim and empty and a rail thin, perky Asian waitress wearing leggings, a lacy pink top and a Santa cap smiles at me over and over like an anime robot. I'm sitting alone in a thin line of red leather banquettes that lead into the lap of a ten-foot golden Buddha. From my vantage point, Buddha doesn't seem to have a penis amidst rolls of sculpted flab. Why would a prophet be obese?

Out on the sidewalk groups of people mince past dancing through a wash of blowing snow. Across the street a store window displays a gigantic bow made up of red lights. Swan is ten minutes late, which is sort of chic. I was fifteen minutes early, which feels a little desperate. I'm sipping my Diet Coke really, really slowly. I decide the waitress could be a zombie. I've never trusted Asian people, which I think makes me a bigot.

I look up to see two young girls in the front window staring in, pointing and laughing. I can feel my face collapsing into a fat little mask of shame and despair. The women have white blond hair, are arm in arm, and are both wearing black fur hats, which accumulate flecks of bright white snow. They are cuddling and laughing and pointing. If I had a gun I would shoot them, like the heroine wife shot so many zombies in the movie.

They knock on the window and wave in my direction. I realize they are communicating with the bony waitress, who stands back by the flabby Buddha. I order another Diet Coke. Snow blows at the window. My iPhone rings and I am suddenly afraid it is Ben. For a terrifying moment I doubt absolutely everything I am doing at this exact moment. It is Swan.

A group of six really large, really black women come in and

argue about where to sit. Swan's voice is soft but hurried.

"I am stuck at a photo shoot. Would you mind coming here?" he says slowly, then sighs long and soft.

The wind snaps at the window. The two happy girls in black fur hats are gone and the black women are arguing loudly. The rail-thin waitress looks like she may start to cry. I jot down the address of Swan's studio which is in a trendy part of downtown called the meat packing district. I pay for my sodas and leave feeling extremely excited and oddly agitated.

I REALLY KNOW nothing about Swan. As I climb a flight of stairs to a space labeled Studio X on a buzzer box below, I imagine that he must be rich. I can't stop a series of candy colored snapshots from presenting themselves as I get near Swan's studio door. He is smiling and blowing out the candles on a birthday cake while I stand at his side; he is astride an elephant wearing Khaki shorts on our fifth anniversary trip to Africa; he is holding a camera and beckoning me.

By the time I reach the landing, the fantasy snapshots have begun to overlap and get muddy and a few of them include Ben, then my father. I wish I had insisted Swan stick to our plan and meet me at the restaurant where I could be poised and ready to tell him about myself and this past four days. The studio door is ajar.

It looks like an elegantly refurbished factory loft. The walls are brick, and four floor-to-ceiling windows line the far wall, looking out onto the street and a rusted sign for ZaZa Meats. There are no blinds or curtains. There are several giant, brutal looking photographic lamps clamped to tall poles. There is a Victorian fainting couch near the entrance, and a small table with a beautiful cut glass pitcher.

Several feet ahead, what I first thought was a statue begins to sway. It is a nude man, dusted white to look like a Greek statue. His hands are tied over his head and he is hanging suspended from a rope pulley. I see him from behind, his back muscles rippling. His ass is very large and stone-like. I am mesmerized and immediately aroused. I think, not of St. Agnes, but of St. Sebastian who was hung up and shot with arrows. I am quickly walking toward this statue man, thinking he may be in distress yet knowing he is a model. This must be a Greek-themed photo shoot of beefy Gods. I want to see his face and his cock before Swan sees me. I'm celibate, after all, and about to fall in love.

As I reach him, his ass cheeks flex. He is able to turn his body slightly so he can sway and see me. His eyes flutter.

"Hurry up," he says in a high voice.

A shutter snaps. Swan has appeared and is taking photos. My cock is hard and standing stiff in the front of my pants and I am horrified, wishing I had stayed at the restaurant. Swan is not going to believe I have been celibate and this entire episode is going to be ruined. My cell phone rings. It is Ben. I turn it off as Swan keeps snapping pictures of me standing near this man dusted white like a granite idol.

I take in Swan's appearance. He still looks mostly as I remember him from our first meeting, very tall, lean and elegant. His movements are still precise. But he is unshaven and wearing only boxer briefs. He is barefoot and his black legs have curly natty hair on them and I swear he is drooling a little out of the corner of his mouth. I think of the zombie movie, imagining that my celibate swan has been infected with a chemical in the water. He is motioning toward the granite man who has begun again to flex his ass muscles.

"Touch him," Swan says.

I imagine this is not Swan, but his evil twin. Swan is bound, gagged and locked in the closet. Unfortunately, this scenario arouses me even more. Four days of no masturbation is having its way with me.

"We can do what we wish with him," Swan says, still shooting pictures and coming closer. "He likes that."

This is not how it is going to happen. This cannot be Swan. I try to figure out what is happening, and in an orderly way I begin to see in my mind how it needs to be for me to stay sane, while at the same time my body does something completely different.

I want: Swan in a suit, sitting on the studio's window ledge in sunlight asking me if he may hold my hand.

And now: I'm placing my hand on the granite ass. White powder is on my palm. The man moans.

"Put your finger there," says Swan gently.

He is beside me now, still taking pictures.

Then back on the ledge: Swan is telling me about his childhood, and what lead to his being celibate and alone. I tell him about my fuck-ups with Ben and we embrace.

And now: The granite man sways as my fingers are probing the clean wet inside of his granite ass and Swan is kissing my neck. Swan's beard stubble cuts at my cheek.

"I knew the first time we met you'd love this," Swan says, so close to me now. "I wanted to surprise you. Disarm you. You like it don't you?"

This last line is spoken in a hard, dark voice that disintegrates my window ledge fantasy and sends me reeling back toward my first meeting with Swan. He said very little and showed no emotion. I created him as I wanted him to be. He was an utter stranger who I recklessly welcomed him into my home to take naked pictures of me. He is no savior. I doubt he was ever celibate and I believe he is on drugs right now. I have been obsessed with him all week and he is really nothing at all.

As Swan yanks down my pants and begins to blow me, I push my face into the granite man's beautiful ass and surrender to a wave of absolute pleasure which eclipses my anxiety, my horror, and my sadness. I am flooded with pleasure and hate. As I arch toward orgasm, I quickly think of a film with Joan Crawford. She was a whore, and a B-actor was cast as a minister to reform her. In the final scene they huddle in a jungle hut during a storm. She weeps, wanting salvation. The minister gives into his animal urges and fucks her. She is broken. I think it was called *Rain*.

The granite man's ass tastes of cinnamon. I cum down Swan's long, black, ugly throat. Looking up, gobbling mouth all wet and oval shaped, he looks like a dirty black swan.

These four days have meant nothing.

I HAVE NEVER wept while biking, but I am crying now, my eyes stinging in the cold as I race at breakneck speed away from Swan and that insane granite ass. I am angry, my rage building so fast and so hard that it forces tears through my narrow lids in this horrific icy wind. I don't feel sad, just vacant and defeated. I am cycling faster than I ever have, weaving through traffic and tearing through red lights. Cars honk and come dangerously close.

I am biking up the West Side, toward Auntie Flora's. I don't care who she thinks I am or how awful she was in the past to my dead mother. I simply want to curl up like a cat at her feet and sleep. Eat sardines on crackers while Lottie reads to us. Fall into a vat of her nutty memories and drift somewhere far off. I can't go home right now.

I park my bike and enter the lobby of Flora's building to find an unfamiliar black man at the reception desk. He is gigantic, with a big bald head, a huge belly, and meaty looking hands holding an unlit cigarette. He is wearing a neatly pressed brown uniform shirt and pants. The regular doorman, a withered little thing who always waves me up without a word has disappeared. There is also a tall Christmas tree standing against the lobby wall near the reception desk. It is green and fake and naked. There are no lights or ornaments, and it looks gaunt, as if it were missing a few of its artificial limbs.

"Do you have the delivery?" the large black man says.

I realize he may have seen me park my bike and is mistaking

me for a messenger. I have never announced myself to Auntie Flora, always just breezed up. I'm not sure what the procedure is, but I give him my information and Flora's apartment number.

"That apartment is vacant," he says.

I glance around, making sure I haven't wandered into the wrong elegant building. He chews the end of the unlit cigarette, staring at me with suspicion.

"Would you call up? I was just there," I say, thinking he's a bit slow and has mixed up the apartment numbers.

"You need to go," he says.

"I am not…"

He cuts me off, still gnawing on that stupid cigarette.

"What's all over your hands?" he says, leaning over the desk toward me to get a better view.

My hands are white with the dusty granite, stained with the fake white crap that made the model look like a statue. I have the hands of a corpse.

The man leans closer and smiles, amused at my confusion. The proximity of his fat face is too much. The thin tether of string holding me to appropriate behavior quivers.

"Listen to me. My aunt is upstairs and is very sick. She's dying and I have her medication and I am going up to see her now," I say.

I am very calm and speak in a steady tone. What is welling up is anguish and rage, but what sputters out of my mouth is super controlled. The lines seem to have had some impact on him. He is dialing a house phone. He is nodding his fat black head, glancing at me, mumbling something, nodding more. Finally he hangs up.

"She's up there. My mistake," he says.

Before I can go up he continues, loudly.

"She doesn't know who you are. Never heard of you. Now you gots ta' go Mister," he says, suddenly revealing a rougher edge, a ghetto touch to his speech. "Don't make me throw your ass out."

A siren wails past out front, red lights swimming across the lobby walls, shadowing the black man's fat face with a deep scarlet glow. I turn and move quickly to the elevator as he glances toward the passing ambulance. I jab the button frantically, suddenly in a ghastly horror film, running from the maniac. But the maniac is me.

He is at me, his chubby hands on my shoulders, pulling me away and out to the curb. He is literally pushing me down, and I fall to my knees on the empty sidewalk. As he retreats I scream.

"Benny. Tell her it's Benny," I scream shrilly, desperately.

The door has shut and a frail old woman is coming up the sidewalk toward me, walking a very skinny dog. The dog sniffs at me and the old woman smiles as if I were a child who'd fallen off his sled.

"Say hi Mr. Muffin," she says to the dog.

She is wearing a white wool coat and a red Hermes scarf. Her dog licks my cheek before they go on. The big black man is watching my every move from the warm lobby doorway. I lie back on the sidewalk, broken and bruised in the cold. I look up but cannot see past the awning to imagined stars. I can hear cars passing. Finally, I get up, unlock my bike and ride away.

december 23

IN THE DARK, half dead, numb after the granite ass-licking incident and that mess with Auntie Flora's retard doorman, I am cruising the internet on my iPhone. Ironically I stumble across a bit of swan trivia on Wikipedia: All swans were thought to be white, until they discovered black swans in Australia in the 18th Century. Now, highly unexpected events are termed "black swans." Good to know.

I am at this moment, lounging very comfortably in my black hole.

I don't know exactly when I slipped in, though undoubtedly during the three-hour bath I took after the long, debasing fuck session with the lying fiend Swan. Wait, let's call him 'The Thing.' I will not justify that loser with an elegant bird's name. I imagine 'The Thing' at this moment, choking to death on a giant elephant-sized granite cock. His cheeks balloon, his eyes explode, his skin turns tar-blue and he disintegrates into dust. This makes me smile.

My black hole loves anger.

In the past I would glimpse my black hole, the tangled edges, the dark interiors, the claws reaching, and I would dash immediately toward sex. This time, I slide in, discovering a soft and smothering muddy substance to sooth my gloom-bitten brain. The thing with Swan irrevocably changed me and I acknowledge this: Swan was a brittle illusion and I was a fool to believe any of it was real; Ben is a lost cause, something I ruined beyond repair months ago; and finally, I am now and always will be absolutely alone. Ruminating on these thoughts, I have been sinking deeper into my black hole with each passing hour. It is giving me an odd strength, this letting go, and I enjoy my slowly building rage. The anger gives me the energy to plot a no holds-barred holiday sex binge.

In celebration, I hang a condom on the December 23rd spot of the advent calendar. It looks like a tiny Santa's bag ready to fill with toys.

I think of men I've recently fucked who I can lure over. I will start with the always eager and available Pig, putting him first on my invite list. He has never refused me. I'd like the binge to last a few days, to include dozens of men and to take me to angry, nasty places that I've never been before. The planning excites me, and gives me the energy to sit up in bed. I text Pig.

free?

Immediately:

yes sir when.

I'm glad my nasty little swine fucker is on the ready. He will never forget this debauchery. I am feeling little jolts of power, like evil electricity zapping its way up my spine. I have a purpose. I am a sexed-up antichrist. Wait, that's too much. Let's just say I will pray at the altar of perversion.

Ben called twice. I'm not going to listen to the voice messages. I cannot risk giving into any stray remnants of emotion. I am cold, like Joan Crawford playing that whore in *Rain*, lost and living alone in the film's last reel.

IN THE MIRROR my ribs pop which is great, but my chest has deflated from a lack of food and exercise, which is unsettling. I don't care about the food part, but my man tits are my big draw. I do three sets of push-ups and they plump a bit.

I know the closer we get to Christmas, the darker and more desperate the city's sex hunters will become. There will be hordes of nameless men, guys living alone or who are Jewish or who are honestly not into the holiday. These men will have lots of free time and will want to do all sorts of very nasty things. They will be lawyers and doctors and trash men and chefs and teachers and drug addicts and actors and security guards. I hope to meet them all.

I've settled into my black hole and decorated it in pleasing shades. It's nice in here. There are no rules in the black hole. I'm committed to getting raw and awful. Reckless. Unsafe. 'Piss in a cup and pour it in you mouth? Sure.' 'Fuck you without a condom? No problem.' 'Stick a rotting cucumber up your ass? Okay.' 'Rape your straight, half-retarded backwoods cousin? Love to.'

I have no conscience. It got lost in the muck.

I've planned a kick-off with Pig, who is on his way over now. I will put the lit tip of a cigarette on the inner curve of his fat ass until he screams. I honestly think he will like this.

My daring attitude makes me smile in my big Ikea mirror. I need to take new nude pictures to post on Manhunt and Grindr, so I relax my face and think angry thoughts. I never take pictures of myself smiling. It's a sexual turn off. I summon my best surly glare, and get a few more shots, then turn around and awkwardly try to snap a decent picture of my ass. I have purchased a 24-hour all access holiday pass on the phone line. I can call at will with no restrictions. My stolen wi-fi connection is working well. I've updated my internet sex sites with a 'join my gang bang' headline.

I sweep and Swiffer mop the floor, in case I get a group and we want to roll around like naughty elves. I hate dust bunnies in my ass. I change the sheets and remove my big comforter so it won't get stained. I have both of my loud fans on, to create that soothing cave feeling. There is one dim light glowing from the bathroom, like a candle deep in a cavern, held by a sole explorer. I'm ready.

"Merry Christmas, motherfucker," I say to my mirror image.

The buzzer blares. Pig is right on time.

I light a cigarette.

december 24

IT'S AFTER MIDNIGHT and I'm thinking of the three prophetic ghosts who visited Scrooge and also of the Three Kings who trudged tirelessly to deliver Gold, Frankincense and Myrrh to the Christ Child. Three is a good number to kick this holiday sex binge into high gear. Pig is here, and a college boy is on the way.

While waiting for the new kid to arrive, I google the month of December hunting for Christmas trivia. Besides Dickens and the Jesus stuff, I stumble across the fact that it's the 'International Day to End Violence Against Sex Workers.' As I fantasize what being violent with a sex worker might look like, I watch Pig spread his whale-pale ass cheeks. The two cigarette burns I inflicted at his arrival flare on either side of his inner buns, blinking like mini-Christmas tree lights. I get up and hang a tiny felt red ribbon on the advent calendar's December 24 spot. I'd like to run out and buy a small tree, but I don't know if I can trust Pig alone here. Plus, he really wants me to fuck him so my cock will chaff the burns and cause more pain. Pig is becoming a bit needy.

My buzzer blares, saving me from those big jolly piglet buns.

I have several super-horny fellows 'on their way soon' from my gang-bang Grindr posting, but this lean little black guy lives a few blocks away and asked if he could pop in for a quickie.

Standing at the peep hole, I think: If I were slightly different, like in a relationship or somehow normal, I might be opening this door to welcome friends to a Christmas party where we listen to carols and sip Eggnog and exchange secret Santa gifts. A memory of my parents involving stockings over a fire place tries to worm its way forward, but I swat it away and focus on the sound of what I guess are dress shoes tapping up the stairs. Pig has lain down on his belly for a quick nap. He looks sort of sweet, which makes me want to hurt him but there's no time.

The black boy steps in and for a moment, there is a rush of wide-eyed shock in his bleary eyes. I touch his agitated crotch and shut the door.

I'VE RARELY SEEN a hairy black boy so I let my palm linger on his tiny round ass which is speckled with natty hair. I inset one finger and press it in and out. He says he's twenty and escaped his Upper East Side family holiday party to go buy cigarettes for his Aunt Sherri. I believe him. His eyes are giant saucers, his mouth wide and clown-like, his body incredibly thin and fit and smattered with that odd curly dark hair. His cock is gigantic.

He insists we watch internet porn. He won't kiss or look at me, but is mesmerized with *Park it in the Rear* where five men in a parking garage have rough anal sex. I think they are using motor oil for lube, which seems ludicrous. He keeps repeating 'this is so hot so hot so hot.' I know the minute I touch his nuts he will cum so I hesitate.

He is moaning as he reaches around and tugs at my cock. Pig is watching us. Ever since I burnt Pig's ass when he first arrived, I have been aware of a slow-building, nagging need for cruelty. I think the fall-out with 'The Thing' and those awful Ben memories has seriously shaken up my shit. It feels sort of hot, the new build of cruel ideas inside of me. But they keep colliding with strangely decorated memories of holidays past, or erratic urges to bake, or hang mistletoe.

As I kiss the black boy's neck, and Pig caresses my back, I wonder what they both would think if I made toll house cookies or suggest we sing "Silent Night" while we fuck. I also wonder if this will be the binge that will overwhelm me with such self-loathing that I will finally off myself. I could lace holiday sugar cookies with a crumbled overdose of Vicodin and sort of eat myself to death.

Pig leans really close to me so I turn and spit on his face. It hits his eyelid in a glob then slowly drools down his cheek like a silky tear. I'd like to hit him.

The black boy is trying to press my stiff cock into his ass.

"I want to feel it, come on," he says breathlessly.

In our initial texts, he said he was negative as did I, but that mean's nothing with tricks. Lying is part of the game. Fucking raw usually means you're drugged, on a suicide mission or HIV positive and don't give a shit. Being the top, it's pretty safe for me to fuck his ass, but as a rule it's not something I do. I never fucked Ben raw during our six months. The black boy is getting greedy, trying to take charge of my cock.

I want to see his face and kiss him before we go forward. He's slid the head of my cock into his tight little hole. It's an incredible turn on, this extra bit of naughtiness. Pig is nibbling my ear as that song about Santa being naughty or nice runs through my head and I pull the black boy's face to me. He resists gamely, whimpering like a child. I grip his cheeks so tight I'm sure I'm leaving a mark as I force him to kiss me. But his eyes are shut.

"Hey," I say sharply.

He snaps open his eyes. They are glassy, like a doll's, and in a split second I see that familiar fuck-trick vacancy, the urgent need to screw harder so your brain can fry so hot that it flies away leaving you numb. I know that at this moment I could be a robot pounding him, that I am not important in the equation of what this kid needs. I kiss him hungrily as he struggles to get away from my mouth. I am completely turned on by forcefully invading the mouth of a kindred fucked-up spirit, and I let my cock slide further into his quivering hole and it feels incredible, smooth and elegant, sliding effortlessly and I suddenly think of my father ice skating one Christmas Eve as my entire body shudders in pleasure and I bite on this black boy's tongue as he screams a name that is not mine.

THERE ARE FIVE of us lounging on my JC Penney blue floral wild tanglewood rug. I moved my two fabric club chairs to the edge of the room to give us space, and am keeping the sofa folded up. I left the blinds open slightly, so we could glimpse the blowing snow outside and be aware of dawn.

The Jew has a horsy face, but nice lips, and is under thirty with a very, very fat cock. He seems happy to be here and willing to do most anything. There is a dark-skinned Mediterranean man with a decent body lying flat on the floor naked, ass in the air. He does not speak and may be asleep. The youngest is clearly on drugs and incredibly thin, but skinny in that youthful wiry way. His tummy is granite-hard to the touch. He is Puerto Rican and angry. He's also very controlling.

And of course there is Pig, who has become a comforting fixture in my house. For a bit, he knelt on all fours so I could use him as a foot stool. I know he will stay with me until the end. We are finishing a short break. The young, drugged one stands and gets things moving again.

"Fuck him, get it in there deep for me," the Puerto Rican tells the Jew, who obliges, gets up and starts rapidly humping the mute Mediterranean on the floor.

This makes the Puerto Rican happy and he grabs me roughly shoving his tongue into my mouth. I can feel his sharp teeth and taste something sweet which makes me think again of toll house cookies. He is opening his mouth so wide that it stretches up to cover my nose and cheeks. He is sucking in my breath and making strange animal noises. I can see out of the corner of my eye the Jew fucking the Mediterranean, bouncing solidly in rhythm on my rug, which thrills but worries me. I wonder if I should have put down plastic. The rug was expensive and I think cum stains will ruin its chic appeal. Pig is slithering across the floor toward us.

Grabbing the back of my head, and keeping his big fish-like mouth locked on my face, the Puerto Rican holds me tight and walks us over to the duo on the floor. He takes tiny steps like a Geisha with bound feet. My stomach rumbles and I realize I haven't eaten in quite a spell.

Holding me firmly, the Puerto Rican straddles the Jew's back and we squat in unison, so he can maintain contact with my mouth while I maneuver my cock into the Jew's ass. Everyone, supposedly, is negative, and I've given up condoms since plowing that silly black boy. Once I dipped into the pool of 'who gives a flying fuck' it was hard to come back. I have to keep reminding myself, also, that this may all end very badly for me, so I might as well live it up.

I'm gasping for air, feeling dizzy, and as I fuck, I think of Jesus being a Jew, and wonder if anyone every fucked him, like one of those sadistic guards that whipped his back with a lash while he carried that awful cross. I'm moving pretty solidly, and the four of us have a nice rhythm as I think again of the horrifying things they did to Jesus before he died. He got back at them, of course, by rising from the dead. I imagine he scared the fuck out of a lot of people who were celebrating his demise. I like Jesus.

I wonder if I could fit twelve men in my studio and we could do a last supper themed gang bang? I suppose that would be better for Easter.

The Jew has started to scream happily. His voice shoots up an octave then he laughs like a female cheetah. The building is nearly empty of tenants this close to Christmas so we can be as loud as we wish. I must have hit his prostate because he is clearly in some sort of ecstasy.

Everyone is cumming at once, which seems pleasant and nicely orchestrated. With my eyes shut I see a mashed-up image of the little drummer boy's moist and funky ass dancing ahead of me, this next to the smooth face of my friend Jesus who has blood tears in his gleeful eyes. I also glimpse a beautiful man I believe to be St. Sebastian and a woman wearing a red and green apron and holding a plate of cookies, as I shoot the latest load of my Christmas binge up the unprotected ass of the Jew. Pig is lying on his stomach, feet in the air, waiting for someone to rub his soft belly.

The room falls silent. After cumming, my thoughts always slide very quickly to a radical dark spot. I chew the inside of my cheek, seeing it as a purple nipple growing out the edge of my now-constant black hole. I believe it will be post-orgasm when I will be most likely to harm myself. Staring at pig, still feeling hungry, I let my anger run free, and imagine him on a platter, apple in mouth, a sharp knife slicing down his center. These new and outrageously violent thoughts can hurt no one. They don't actually exist. I think of the classic novel *Lord of the Flies*. I am pretty certain there was a character named Piggy. I think they killed him.

I seriously wonder if I could ever kill someone, other than myself, that is, which doesn't count.

I WAKE AND the four men are listless on the floor, and for a moment I wonder if they are dead. Snoring tells me otherwise. I imagine forcing a can of Pam cooking spray up Pig's ass as he sleeps. I could spray him up there, like lube. Sex, violence, and holiday baking thoughts are really colliding a lot.

I turn on the TV, keeping the volume muted. Bugs Bunny is dancing, wearing heels and a red wig. He's applying lipstick.

The Puerto Rican bolts up and screams, "Shit, he got it up in me!"

He puts a hand to his forehead, blinks several times, then turns to register me and Bugs Bunny. He stands, unsteadily on one then another skinny foot as he wakes. His cock bobs big and pretty. He swoops at me and falls to his knees, planting a kiss on my neck. I switch the channel to a dancing snowman. He is wearing a top hat, singing, and leading cartoon children down a holiday avenue. It's really sweet, but also sad for some unknown fucking reason. I want to sing along.

"I love him," the Puerto Rican says, and I think he means the snowman but I can't be sure.

JAMIE IS AN escort who will bring our gang-bang number to six. I message-chat with him on Manhunt, recalling that today is 'End Violence Against Sex Workers Day.' I don't bring that up.

His many profile pictures are calendar-like: tall, oiled and sculpted body, square jaw, Midwest handsome wearing a wrestling singlet, then a fireman's hat, then a thong and finally sheer white bike shorts. Despite his raging beauty, he sounds lost. Over the phone, he say's he's bored, has no clients, and is eating a second tub of Ben & Jerry's 'Chunky Monkey' ice cream. He has a tiny lisp. I'm certain he's dumb, jaded and has always felt useless. He probably ran away at sixteen and has been abused for years. I fantasize about all the men that have treated him very, very badly and it's a serious turn on. I bet he's been raped, beaten, slugged and had a bat shoved up his ass. The longer this binge continues, the higher I have to set the bar on my personal cruelty stakes. Hitting Pig just isn't enough anymore. I'm slowly morphing into a real bad ass mother fucker.

I buzz Escort Jamie up and he bursts into our group wearing head-to-toe purple spandex, like some holiday superhero or a professional speed skater. His cock-package is sculpted and rises like an azure mountain. From behind, he offers two perfect half moon melons. All of us perk up, save for the Mediterranean who is still lying face down on the floor. Pig is giggling and I wonder if the Puerto Rican fed him drugs.

The Puerto Rican attacks our new member from behind, the Jew in front, both pressing lips to chilly lavender spandex mounds. I go in for a kiss and can taste the recently devoured Chunky Monkey ice cream, all banana and chocolate and icy preservatives. We hover around Jamie, guiding him into the room, licking and tonguing him. He is our unexpected vision, the angel on our gang-bang tree top. I feel a tensing in Jamie's jaw so I pause. He quite suddenly lurches away from me, from all of us, and in one elegant burst he vomits on my kitchen floor. A puddle of yellow goo begins to dribble toward the Mediterranean.

I guide Jamie to the sofa, then run to fetch a towel to stop the vomit from trailing to my expensive tanglewood rug. By the time I return, the Jew and the Puerto Rican are positioned at either end of Jamie, yanking off his spandex suit, both wildly aroused. He is not resisting, and everyone seems to be oblivious to the overpowering sweet, sickly scent of regurgitated banana funk. The line of yellow liquid has reached the face of the Mediterranean, puddling near his nose on the floor. I nudge him with my foot and he turns over, eyes shut, smiling. I want to kick him hard but I resist. I get down, naked, on all fours to mop up the yellow crap before it can wreck my rug, then I toss the towel into the kitchenette and return to the fun.

Jamie is naked on the sofa, arms over his head, cheek turned to one side, posed like St. Sebastian in my vision, awaiting penis-arrows to pierce his pale and perfect skin. He is an alluring specimen. I like that he is so beautiful and so fucked up. I get atop him, struggling to fit on the crowded sofa. We all tumble down onto the tanglewood rug.

Jamie settles on his stomach, ass in the air, and I get ready to mount him. The Puerto Rican joins me atop Mount Jamie and with a little help from the Jew, who is yanking Jamie's ass cheeks apart, we both insert our cocks and begin to double fuck him. This is another item to add to my ten things to do before I die list. I've only seen this in a porno, never experienced it.

The Mediterranean and Pig are cuddling near us, watching, and I imagine they will pull out a big tug of movie popcorn to share. They are actually a cute couple.

We have found our fuck rhythm, and I'm kissing the Puerto Rican, both of us sweating. Jamie's body begins to bounce with the force and I get a quick glimpse of his face, turned against the floor his eyes and mouth wide open and I think he is trying to speak.

He gasps loudly and in my rising pleasure I become acutely aware that I know that face, that widening of the mouth, that moment before a scream. Jamie turns his increasingly terror-stricken face to me, and I clearly see myself turning my face toward the camera in that tent when I was nine, feeling that older boy's cum on my stomach and the hot explosion of his camera flash in my face.

I feel that millisecond mash-up of fear and shame and excitement so searing it's like skate blades slicing into my retina. I am near cumming when Jamie's bleary eyes meet mine and my nine year old eyes too and I am sure Jamie is in a state of terrible pain and panic and wants me to stop, but the cum is already sliding up my inner cock shaft toward sex nirvana so I ignore Jamie's horror and let that shot build further before giving into a blow of utter regret, yanking out and knocking the Puerto Rican off of this abused kid who can't get out enough air to scream stop.

Cum is still leaking out of my cock which is shuttering open and closed in post orgasm and I feel ill with fever as I crawl to Jamie to cradle him, to pet him, and for one crazy second to absolutely love him. I think he may be the one.

His skin is hot to my touch and I press my ear to his mouth so he can tell me, so he can say it, and he does, but not really.

"Why did you stop?" he whispers.

I roll away, as far away as I can. My black hole blankets me and I sleep.

I'VE LOCKED MYSELF in the bathroom with my white box of journals and some wooden, red tipped stove matches. The mute Mediterranean finally left, but Pig, the Puerto Rican, Jamie and the Jew are still going strong. I have the Ben journals piled in the tub and the match poised but I am unable to do it. My plan to meet and make peace with Ben completely dissolved once I started this whole gang bang. But I can't seem to light my past on fire and watch it turn to ash. I suppose once this is done, all hope will be gone and I'll be faced with really ending it all, which is pretty damn depressing. I don't think I can have any more sex with this group. There is no reason to prolong the inevitable.

I sigh and call Pig into the room. He's become such a comfort to me.

He doesn't need words, he knows me so well, my Pig. He sees the journals and the matches and he intuits what to do. His hands, though, are sweaty and trembling so he keeps dropping the kitchen matches. I can't help but want to light one and try to burn Pig's ass cheeks again. But that's all over. I have to move on.

After the fourth match, Pig finally gets the thing lit. He drops the match and it immediately goes out. He is perplexed and in the lull I am suddenly having second thoughts about all of this. I can see the edge of the Pink Skeleton Head notebook and I see that picture I took of Ben on New Year's Eve peeking out at me. It looks like the edge of his lips, trying to crawl out of the soon to be demolished journal. Those lips want to say something to me, I'm sure. I realize burning these memories is like killing Ben, and I choke up, dizzy and in one of those awful moments of dread, know that this is a really bad idea. Pig, however, has finally found his way with the matches, and is bending down with two lit at once, pressing the flame to paper as it starts to catch.

What I do next I see happening for a split second in my mind, before I actually do it. It's like this: I pull Pig up to his feet, flaming matches still in hand. I grab his wrist and with all of my might, I snap his wrist backward so it touches his forearm, popping. The matches go out and Pig squeals in outrageous pain. His eyes are looking directly at me and I realize he has never looked straight at me like this. He has pretty green eyes and a look of utter terror. His broken wrist is lying limply backwards on his forearm, dangling.

I realize I have actually accomplished this. It was not just a flash in my mind. I did this thing.

The other three have joined us, the Jew, the Puerto Rican, and Jamie and everyone is yelling as I step back and sit on the toilet. Pig is screaming and the three men, who minutes ago were depraved sex fiends, have become caring nurse-like people, looking at me with true hate and disgust, helping Pig into the other room to dress so they can all leave. To the hospital I guess.

His hand really does look horrible and as they go, I think of the zombie movie and all of those yanked-off and chewed-up limbs. This is nothing compared to that. They mustn't have seen the film or they wouldn't make such a big deal out of one mangled wrist.

I am left alone.

THE STOVE IS smoking because I've burnt the toll house cookies I baked in an attempt to restore normalcy after breaking

Pig's wrist. I throw the hot cookie sheet into the sink and watch it steam under cold water. The burnt dough dissolves into gut-like mud. I can't bear to deal with any of this mess. The apartment has blown to pieces and I think of the picture of the *USS Shaw*, in flames at Pearl Harbor. The advent calendar has fallen to the floor and is missing felt toys. There's a used condom lying on the top of a little train caboose near December 22. Everything stinks of burnt dough, piss and musky sex. I have to get out of here.

I DON'T KNOW what time of day it has become. I'm going out because I need to see people and come up with a final plan. My stomach has tied itself into a neat little knot. I keep thinking of angels and reindeer and sex workers and sailors and soldiers and pilots and bloody zombies as I stumble down the stairs to the street.

It is very late at night. I can tell because there is no traffic, few people. The wind is biting and cold. The light of my neighborhood deli burns brightly and I think of Mary and Joseph, tromping through some terrifying countryside, searching for a place to rest and I want so much to rest. My brain is absolutely scarred.

There is a shield of hanging plastic, like a shrouding tarp, around the entrance to the deli. It protects a line of petite Christmas trees and flowering red plants. Through the snapping plastic, the light from inside the deli is muted and beautiful. I stand outside and enjoy the extreme cold. I am trembling. The bitter cold is slightly eradicating the creeping sadness that began to build the minute the picture of Ben fell out of the Skeleton Head journal and after I broke Pig's wrist.

My bike is parked in front of the deli and instead of entering, I go to my yellow Huffy, unlock it and mount. My body is shivering and I want to keep this up, to take myself further. I realize I've filled my tub, my sacred hot lavender hiding place, with those horrible journals. I'm not going back there.

As I pedal my bike across the avenue, pressing my crotch hard into the seat, I drive toward something that can make sense of all of this. Or at least distract me until I can figure out what the fuck I am going to do to myself, or to someone I hate. Something utterly off balance and insane. Like Santa fucking a reindeer to death, or an elf having unprotected self with a rag doll. These weird thoughts make me smile, as I bike toward Auntie Flora's house. I need to know that she still exists and that she knows who I am.

AS I CYCLE across West End Avenue, the moon dangles above like a milky ornament in the night sky. The trees along the street are drooping and silvery with heavy ice. Far down below is the Hudson River. My tires slide, as I skid through a wet spot, but I right myself and lock my bike, my hands already numb in front of Auntie Flora's place.

The regular doorman is back in place, which is a good sign. The fat black man must have been a temp. He smiles at me, one hand waving and the other cradling a steaming mug with a snowflake on the front. His head droops, and I think of the frayed Santa ornament on my advent tree. This doorman and I have never said a word to one another.

"You're such a good boy to visit her," he says, slurring as I enter the lobby. "It's just too bad."

He doesn't look at me, just keeps staring into his mug like he's reading holiday tea leaves so I move swiftly to the elevator and up to Auntie Flora. The elevator is empty, save for lacy gold garland curling around the top of its four boxy walls. I don't know what I expect to find here. My last two visits were quite disturbing.

Auntie Flora, however, is the only person I know to run toward for any kind of comfort. She's old so she must know something. I think of Pig, believing that he could understand and console me, if only I hadn't snapped his wrist in half. I can't go back to my place, all loose cum and burnt cookie dough. Disgusting.

I suck in a breath in the elevator but am strangled with the thought that this senile old cow is the only real family I have. I manage a very lame gasp in, then out, as I leave the elevator and summon the courage to gently tap on her door at this insane hour on Christmas Eve. I tap and immediately a voice calls to me. The door is unlocked.

Inside, the overhead light is soft, dim and red, and I think both of a Mexican bordello and of Rudolph's blinking nose. The living room is crowded with boxes and in the scarlet glow I step toward a wonderland where I am six again and my parents have filled our rattling farm house with misshapen, cheaply wrapped boxes of toys. I recall ripping into a bike and a set of encyclopedias. Flora will turn to me at any second, my new Auntie Mame, cheerful in a red velvet dress, pulling me into her warm bosom. Instead, she coughs and I hear the rattle of ice cubes in a tumbler.

The boxes are brown and ugly. They are moving boxes.

"I knew you'd come. Lottie said you never called her back today but I was sure," Flora says, not rising at all as I imagined, rather falling further back into her favorite chair, drink in hand, eyes wide in disbelief.

She speaks slowly and clearly, and I think she is lucid.

"It happened so quickly. The stocks, the investments, down the drain. I never imagined they'd find a buyer for the apartment like that but thank heavens they did or I just don't know what would happen. It's barely tolerable, all gone just like that," she says, lifting her gnarled, spotted hand in an effort to snap and accentuate the thought.

There is no snap, only a heaving sigh as she lies her head back again on the chair cushions.

"Come sit," she says, indicating the stool near her.

I don't want to go to her. I am insanely tired and lost and am guessing what this all means for me in terms of money and inheritance. I don't, at this moment however, know what else to do. So I sit.

On the stool, I am beneath her, and she reaches over and touches my chin, lifting my face to her. She has never touched my face before, only my hand. And she has never looked so clear and concerned.

"Why are you alone tonight? What have you done?" she says.

Her hand is like balm on a stinging burn.

"I broke a man's hand," I say softly.

"This is not the night to break a man's heart. That is unforgivable," she says, still holding my chin. "But we mend. I nearly broke your parent's marriage. That is my unforgivable."

She slumps again, and releases my chin. I have become miniscule on this tiny stool and feel as dimensional as the flat ornaments hanging on my advent calendar. There is nothing between my bones.

Fuck, this is depressing.

"What do you mean?" I say because I want to hear myself speak, and somewhere deeply hidden in my brain is the recognition that she may reveal something about my parents that I never knew.

"You were at camp when it happened," she says.

What wells up and spits out of me is automatic and vile.

"I was not at camp, I was never at camp. I am an only child," I say very quickly.

I have suddenly decided that I am not putting up with this shit. She needs to step up. I have nothing to lose, as my fantasy inheritance seems to be dissolving like the ice cubes in the old bat's high ball glass. I stare at her old face and realize I am angry, but also very glad she is here. I want to touch her.

She lifts her head and considers me. She studies me for a moment then leans forward.

"You were always in trouble. You are the nasty little shit

aren't you," she says with a flush of recognition.

She throws her head back laughing loudly. She laughs steadily for several moments, bits of drool slipping out of the sides of her mouth and down her withered chin. I think of a fairy tale witch, and also of my cum globing on Pig's chin last night.

Someone is creeping on soft feet up the hallway and it could be the ghost of my mother or it could be Santa Claus or the devil but it is likely Lottie. I wait for her snort.

"It was that awful summer and you were at," Flora looks down at me on my stool, struggling for a moment. "All right you were in the barn. We all knew what you did out there you dirty thing."

My face is shattering into many shameful pieces. Nobody knew anything. I made sure of that. She is wrong.

"I don't know why I cut into her," she says. "I don't know what made me do it."

"You were drunk," I say.

There is a soft snort from the hall and a wild, young crazy laugh from Flora, as she sits up straight in her chair.

"I was drunk yes and I still am," she says, lit up now, brightening the dim red room with an old woman's final mania. She sits erect and launches fast.

"I called them in like I owned the place. It was their home. Theirs. I sat them down and I tore into them. His wasted life. Her neediness. How she ruined him. Dragged him away off to that stinky farm. Away from what I had dreamed for him, away from his real family."

Flora laughs again, but softer then goes dim and quiet, the flaring candle of her suddenly snuffed.

"Course he wanted to go. He ran to get away from us, I knew. Why *she* didn't know is what's nuts. But she believed me. She dragged herself up the stairs. Locked away."

There are no more snorts from the hall, but I hear feet shuffling. I think this will all be set aside soon. Flora will be made to go limp and quiet.

"He told me to leave and never come back," she says,

Diary of a Sex Addict 143

bringing her hand up with a magical wave. "And now I have to go again. Paris. Everything is just dwindling away."

I suddenly recall a forgotten moment with my parents that summer, after all that drunken drama with Flora. It was after she had left and things had settled down. I had snuck out of bed and was headed out to the barn to masturbate, thinking the house was dead asleep. I used the back door, so as not to be heard, then came around front past the porch. I saw the living room light on which was strange. I crept onto the porch, then close to the front window which was open wide in the heat. My parents were sitting stiffly across from one another, whispering in angry tones. I leaned into the window to better hear their gentle anguish. I knew, hearing them, they were protecting me, speaking in a hush so as not to wake me. They were quiet and sad looking, and my mother's head was bowed. My father stood up and went to her, sat by her, his shoulders heaving with a sigh as he awkwardly took her hand. I felt, standing there, that I was a secret appendage and part of them and I knew there would never be flight. They would always stick it out, work things through, stay together and die together. That's what good people do. It comforted me deeply back then, in that moment, on the porch. It seemed to erase the deeper, lingering terror that Auntie Flora had brought into the house.

I suppose at that point, I expected I'd be like them. Steady and true like that. I had not gone out to the barn that night, but crept back up to my room and slept, comforted by the sounds of my parents shuffling up to bed. But that comfort, that sensation dissolved long ago. I have never stuck anything out, never been steady and true, never been anything but a big fat sex addict. Not with Ben, not in love or lust or sex. Everything has been disposable to me, which is pretty awful and right now it seems, impossible to change.

"You must come see us in Paris," Lottie says.

I know I will never go to Paris. Auntie Flora is struggling to stand, ready to open her arms and give me a farewell hug. As she stretches out her fat little hand to me I see Pig's hand snapping back like a folding piece of paper and the terror in his eyes. I could do the same thing right now to Flora. I could harm her like she harmed my mother. I could twist off her doll-like head before she escapes with all my vague hope of inheritance and redemption. I could do something really horrible, something that would make it into the papers. But then, really, there is nobody left that would notice.

I am entirely vacant inside and think this is what Oprah would call the moment when all hope is lost. On television, something happens at this cliff hanging crux to yank the lost soul backwards. There is no hand reaching out to save me, only the backward flying fist of pig, and my ugly fantasies of maiming my aunt.

I have had enough.

Auntie Flora is speaking, telling me something about a gift but I have already pressed quickly past Lottie and am out the door, into the elevator, past the drunk doorman, into the street, back to myself where I can try to breathe more deeply and end this torture.

Flora, like Swan Man, and really like my parents, was a barely lit flame in my torrid little life. I mount my bike and push toward something that is finally mean, brutal, harsh, and deadly. An ending. Thank God. I'm so tired.

I will go to Central Park.

THE STREETS ARE deserted, the moon a curling sickle in the crystal black night sky. The city has shuttered itself, softened for a moment. The air is icy but I'm not bothered, I've moved past that first numbing irritation. As I bike down toward the Park, my throat opens wide with the mean ice-wind. I breathe deeply as my hard belly heaves. I love this riding, this midnight escape. The street is lined with elegant, dark brownstones. The front windows glow mysteriously with the subdued light of Christmas trees that sit beyond thick silk curtains.

I cross East and the icy sidewalk trees shimmer. The expensive bath shops and pastry bars are shuttered and dead. I imagine a cluster of lost, beautiful men hiding in the park, their cum spurting out and freezing mid air then slicing into me with daggers of death.

As I pedal, I think: I am one dramatic fucker.

My cheeks are tingling. The whispered city legends of late night Central Park sex and brutal murder have softened over the years. Still, no sane person enters the park after dark. Late-night joggers still occasionally get raped or sliced up. I'm at the East side entrance. A lone bus slouches past, then the street is vacant. This is my moment of clarity, where I turn back, find warmth, applaud my moment of insanity but realize I won't go through with my death wish.

Instead I think: It's time to finish this. Just do it asshole.

The winding park road pulls me into its black belly, gladly sucking out all this anguish and spitting me into a new breath of madness. I ride swiftly, fiercely into the park. It is bleak and empty and I think of my black hole, realizing I have finally entered it, found the center where I will sink and drown. This isn't how I imagined it, but what the fuck? Life is like that.

I ride past the East Side lake that is dotted with lazy canoes in summer but is now dreary. I continue up the hill past a shuttered snack bar into the Rambles. The Rambles are a winding patch of footpaths, meant for bird-watching but famously claimed in the 1960s by gay men for secret fucking. I'm walking my bike now and I can only hear the sound of the whipping wind. Ahead, past a gnarled dead tree, there is a mild rise in the path. The rise borders a little ravine, and I see a light. I am completely numb with cold and my eyes burn with some nameless emotion. I suppose this could be it, the end, or something.

I never did come up with ten things to do before I die. Too late now.

At the tip of the tiny ravine I see them clustered around a trash can, and past them, from my vantage point I can see the lip of one of the park's biggest lakes, frozen and misty. Wood, twigs and paper are lit in the trash can the men huddle near, smoke snaking up and making the view of the lake in the distance fill for a moment with phantom images of forgotten skaters. My father is skating elegantly, and way beyond I see myself as a boy sitting and wearing my bear mittens.

I creep closer to the bum scene, when one of them very near the flaming trash can pushes his pants off and is immediately overtaken. In the fire light, as the smoke obliterates the lake in the background, I can see the man is wearing leather and his ass is very big, hard and muscled. I step forward, then slip and slide down the little hill toward the burning trash can. The smallest man in the cluster, who is watching the fucking group, turns and eyes me. He looks like a gnome, bushy and small. His hair is ratty, his skin brown and dirty. He is dressed in layers of ragged cloth. He gets close to me, and I can see how thick his eyebrows are and that he has friendly, curious eyes. He is sniffing a thumb-sized bottle of amyl nitrate poppers.

"Shit, you hot," he says, offering the bottle of poppers to me.

I take a snort and feel a flood of warmth and dizziness, my brain colliding with the scene and my overall plan. I'm giddy from the sickly smelling poppers. The gnome takes my hand, almost gently, and leads me to the fire.

"You gotta stay close or you gonna freeze crazy motherfucka," he says.

The men are bound tightly, sharing the leather man's ass and I can see they are not bums at all, but fairly attractive, possibly drugged white men. A tall black man stands nearby drinking from a frosty beer bottle. I'm still dizzy from the poppers. The gnome steps closer to me.

"What you up to fucker?" he says, snorting the poppers again. "I'm Harry. They call me Popper-head Harry cause I sniff my poppers all night. Keeps my blood hot."

Diary of a Sex Addict

The lure of danger has softened and I again wonder if I can go through with this. These men don't look terribly dangerous, and I'm guessing there is not a maniacal killer amidst them which is disappointing. I fear I may be the most unhinged person in the group. Great.

Harry holds onto my hand, like he's leading a child to the edge of a cliff. We both watch the men near the flaming can fuck and grind. The trash can radiates a good deal of heat. The tall, beer drinking black man steps forward and feeds the fire with wood then smiles at me. He looks oddly familiar and I wonder if I have had him to my apartment to screw. I am thawing and when I turn to look at Harry, who is still inexplicably holding my hand, he stares deeply. He is disastrously broken, yet seemingly resigned, which makes me smile. He releases my hand and reaches toward my pants, but I gently brush him away. He grunts, then snorts more poppers as I step very close to the trash can. For a second I run my hand through the flame. The leather man has fallen to the ground bellowing in orgasm. A few of the men are eyeing me now with interest. A large white guy wearing an unusually expensive looking suit stumbles toward me. Harry steps in.

"He ain't available. We together, him and me," he says, attempting to take ownership.

I find his attitude funny and touching and take the poppers from Harry and snort deeply. As I lean my head back my glimpse of the moon in the cloudless sky seems terribly profound, like it means something that I will never grasp. I will die without ever really learning anything from this crap. My nose burns from the poppers but I want more. Someone is caressing my ass. It is the tall black man, now massaging me from behind as I take another snort from the poppers bottle. The black man has reached his arm around to undo my pants and I let him, because this is the shit I came for. Harry is grumbling and steps away leaving me with his prized poppers.

The flame from the trash can shoots up with a burst of

newspaper that Harry has dropped in. I feel the heat on my naked ass. The black man is bending down and spreading my cheeks and shoving his tongue in, which is warm and comforting, and another man from the group is coming toward me. I am protected by the men and there is an overwhelming warmth. I see Harry yanking on his hair, pulling out small pieces and tossing nappy strands angrily at the fire. He's cussing and pointing his finger at me as I snort more poppers and push my ass back into a tongue and turn my cheek for a wet kiss and for a second the black cheek on mine is Swan, and we are in love. Then I remember what a shit he is and that all goes away.

Harry is pissed. I imagine he thinks I used him and tossed him aside, which is true, because that's what I do. I want to tell gnome Harry that this is who I am. I like it this way. I wonder if he's carrying a knife. He might slice me up in a popper-fueled rage. Doubtful.

I'm sliding back to sit on the black man's face because my legs won't hold me anymore. My back is arching, my waist thrusting forward to meet a face and I turn my head to imagine a mist rising over the lake, where elegant skaters layered in fur and hot wooly bear mittens skid past one another, never touching. This, I think, is not the inside of my black hole. This is something else. For a moment I miss my parents and wish they had lived a bit longer.

I pull away from the black man's tongue and turn on him.

"Fuck me," I say.

I rarely get fucked, so the pain of insertion is likely to shift my mood back to the black hole, back to despair and pain and death thoughts. The black man is guiding me to the ground and there are two of them behind me, both wanting my ass. I feel him push in and the pain is piercing, but not for long. The cold ground on my face is very distracting, and once he gets into a rhythm it actually starts to feel really good. I guess I've been missing something all of these years. I think of my list. Things to do before I die. Get fucked with pleasure. That brings my list to six.

The black man pulls out and someone else is mounting me and I pray to God it's not that ugly gnome Harry, though I have little control. Someone is leaning on my back, keeping me down and the one inside me now hurts a bit. It must be larger. My cheek is starting to feel numb on the cold ground so I shut my eyes and wonder if anyone has ever been fucked to death.

december 25

THERE IS A brilliant sun and a great deal of warmth. I can't force my eyes open yet I see in the distance a fiery little fairy dancing across a bank of clouds. This is the other side. I've done it.

An awful burning sensation and a cramp in my right ass cheek tells me otherwise. The sun is bright, but the cold remains and I'm lying face down in a ravine, alone, in Central Park. I am obviously not dead. No maniacs, no killers, no fucking to death. I am disappointed, angry, relieved.

My fingers are frost bitten and burn like fuck. I did not wear gloves, which makes sense since I thought this was a suicide mission. My finger tips are blue and numb and my whole body aches and is burning in a rotting freezer burnt meat sort of way. I stand, then lick my fingers which does not help. My ass really hurts. I'm bleeding down there. I look for my bike but it's gone. At least there was a capable thief in the crowd. This comforts me. I imagine that little gnome Harry with the poppers cycling happily around Manhattan. Merry Christmas, little sex gnome.

I climb out of the ravine feeling about a hundred and ten. The lake is in the distance and I walk toward it. The sky is clear and there is an attractive young couple, bundled in layers of knitted wool and cashmere, walking hand in hand. They wave to me and I imagine I must look homeless or psycho. I growl at them as they pass but they seem un-phased.

At the edge of the lake I have one final chance. I can walk out to the center, crash through the thin ice and fairly quickly freeze and drown. Isn't this what I've dreamed of, drowning myself in my tub, calculating how to do it, sliding into the black hole forever on the wings of a Vicodin cocktail? Some marvelous people have drowned themselves, Virginia Woolf, Spalding Gray. Or did he hang himself?

What I honestly want, though, is a cup of really hot, really strong Starbucks coffee. I suddenly think again of Joan Crawford in that movie and try to recall what she did once the pastor fucked her and her world collapsed. She was in front of her hut, in the jungle. The pastor sulked away, head down in shame. The camera pulled away slowly leaving her alone, a broken woman, and she started to laugh. The camera moved further and further away as she laughed louder and louder and louder, hysterically, as the music swelled.

I try to laugh but my throat is too tight. I really want that cup of hot Starbucks coffee. I rub my stinging hands together and feel life there, then I sit down at the lakeside, in a little bunch of frozen leaves. The leaves are like a tiny throne and I remember that I used to sit on a pile like this wearing my bear mittens, watching my father soar around the ice with his buddies. I don't recall being cold back then. My mother undoubtedly bundled me in a big sweater and wooly coat. I could really use those fucking bear mittens about now. A swan has skidded onto the lake, pausing, then with great effort wrenching its wings up, only to waddle forward. It is not a swan, of course, it is a frigid old duck.

The sun makes the lake shimmer, just like the tiny glass pond in the Lord & Taylor holiday window I saw this month. There was a little girl that tried to push through that window. I feel miniscule, child-like and wonder what my parents would think of their son, now, sitting on the edge of all of this. I've clearly done things they would never have imagined. Sordid things, true, but not without a sense of adventure and gumption. My father used to love to talk about his father, who ran from the Nazis in Germany and trekked to the Missouri World's Fair. My father spoke in hushed, awe rich tones of that journey. Perhaps, looking at me, he'd be mildly impressed by my insanity. Not everyone can survive a night of wild, random fucking in Central Park. There is something to be said for that.

I realize I'm thinking like someone else, not the 'me' prior to this past year's sexual descent, and not the violent, distraught creature that busted Pig's wrist. Not the boy me in bear mittens enraptured by my skating father, and not the calculating me lying to Ben. Not even the typist me at the Domestic Violence clinic jacking off in the restroom.

I don't quite know who this latest me is, but staring into the lake, I think he is going to reveal himself in a flourish. The wretched old duck has stopped moving, and is batting its tattered wings rapidly and I think 'what is that thing doing?' and more, 'what am I doing?' and 'what was Ben, Swan or Pig to me?' And as always, I default to 'I don't know,' but as that creature works to maneuver its weighty, gossamer silk wings I think 'But I did know. There was a millisecond with each of those men when I did know. And that will come back.' Ideally, this will not happen on my deathbed.

I stand, unsteadily, in awe of both death and life, and think simultaneously of Jesus Christ and Joan Crawford and wonder if they have met. My body is shaking. I'm laughing. Maybe Joan wasn't hysterical at the end of that movie. Maybe she was just taking it all in stride. Maybe she was meeting her true slut self.

I begin to trudge forward, not slouching toward Bethlehem, just walking to the nearest Starbucks. My body aches with each step but I am a little less cold and I believe, quite certainly, that my black hole has dried up. Like a puss filled abscess on a dead bandit's ass, or a back wood's Louisiana swamp that one day miraculously empties itself to reveal a pit of missing animal bones. The remnants are there, the edges remain, but all the mystery and power and drama become shapeless and dusty.

Crossing 5th Avenue, I check my iPhone. I have a bunch texts from my reclusive friend Michael, the last being *where the fuck are you asshole? merry xmas*. He is a sweetheart.

I can see Starbucks a few blocks up and catch a glimpse of myself in a Lincoln Town car window. Other than my gnarled hands, a few smears of mud on my face and twigs in my hair, I look pretty good. I could probably pick someone up at Starbucks, have sex in the john. I realize I've said this out loud, because a very elegant old woman has halted behind me. She's wearing a white cashmere coat, an Hermes red silk scarf with gold coins raining across it, a gorgeous Jill St. John wool skirt and pretty black leather shoes with gold buckles. She is walking a very skinny dog, which I recognize. It is Mr. Muffin and he licked my cheek a few nights ago as I lay on the sidewalk in front of Auntie Flora's after having been manhandled by the doorman. Today, he wears a big red bow around his pencil-thin neck. I swear he is smiling at me. I wish he would come to me.

"I'm sure you could," she says with an odd smile. "Merry Christmas."

She moves on and I notice a tiny swagger in her old hips, a proud thrust to her withered shoulders and a shake to her Jill St. John covered backside. Old money I guess, and certainly a slut. Trailing the pair, I snap a picture, her ass swaying, Mr. Muffin's ass swaying. I email it to Michael.

I follow her until I hit Starbucks, then I go inside.

about the author

An award-winning writer, SCOTT ALEXANDER HESS has written fiction which has appeared in the *Thema Literary Journal* and *Omnia Revitas Review*. *Diary of a Sex Addict* is his second novel; his first, *Bergdorf Boys*, was serialized in *Ganymede Journal* and will soon be released by JMS Books LLC. He is working on another novel set in rural Arkansas and New York City circa 1918. His screenplay, *Tom in America*, is being produced by Queens Pictures in 2012.

Scott has contributed to various national magazines, including *Genre, OutTraveler*, and *Instinct*. Scott is a MFA graduate of The New School. For more information, please visit his website at scottalexanderhess.com.

Printed in Great Britain
by Amazon.co.uk, Ltd.,
Marston Gate.